About the Author

Janet Dorey was born and raised in Halifax, Nova Scotia. She worked as Administrative Assistant within the Faculty of Medicine, Dalhousie University for twenty-five years, and is now happily retired. Art, rug-hooking, gardening, grandchildren, and dreaming up stories with colourful characters quite easily fill her days. *At The Drop of a Tomato* is her first literary work.

At The Drop of a Tomato

Janet Dorey

At The Drop of a Tomato

Olympia Publishers
London

www.olympiapublishers.com
OLYMPIA PAPERBACK EDITION

Copyright © Janet Dorey 2023

The right of Janet Dorey to be identified as author of
this work has been asserted in accordance with sections 77 and 78 of
the Copyright, Designs and Patents Act 1988.

All Rights Reserved

No reproduction, copy or transmission of this publication
may be made without written permission.
No paragraph of this publication may be reproduced,
copied or transmitted save with the written permission of the publisher,
or in accordance with the provisions
of the Copyright Act 1956 (as amended).

Any person who commits any unauthorised act in relation to
this publication may be liable to criminal
prosecution and civil claims for damage.

A CIP catalogue record for this title is
available from the British Library.

ISBN: 978-1-80439-158-7

This is a work of fiction.
Names, characters, places and incidents originate from the writer's
imagination. Any resemblance to actual persons, living or dead, is
purely coincidental.

First Published in 2023

Olympia Publishers
Tallis House
2 Tallis Street
London
EC4Y 0AB

Printed in Great Britain

Dedication

For my brother, Wayne

Acknowledgements

A heartfelt thank you to my enthusiastic readers who have either provided feedback on specific sections, or read the final draft in its entirety. Alan, Anne, Anna, Bev, Brodie, Cindy, Colleen, Craig, Debbie, Deborah, Des, Dilly, Joyce, Judy, Kate, Nina, Pam, Sandy, Sandi, Sara, Wes, Maggie and Pat.

CHAPTER 1

Burnt toast and a familiar edginess hung in the air as young Matthew shuffled into the kitchen. "Aw, c'mon, you two, not this again," he said as he slid the carton of orange juice from the refrigerator.

"Now, son," said Dan. "I was just talking to your mom about—"

"I know, Dad. It's all we ever hear... this crap."

"Rats were in the trash again," said Dan. "Look at the mess," he said pointing to the lower cupboard. "Chewed straight through the floor!"

Tipping the carton to his lips, the boy shrugged. "So what? Cities have rats. Live with it, Dad."

His mother, Karla, snatched a glass from the shelf and shot across the worn linoleum floor. "How many times!" she said. "Use a glass!" Karla too had grown weary of Dan's old pitch – small town life and clean ocean air would be beneficial to their health. They'd have a charming country home, eat from a flourishing vegetable garden, and cut through ocean swells on a sleek little sailboat.

"Oyster Bay would be only an hour's commute to work," said Dan.

"Get a move on, Matt," Karla said. "You'll be late for school."

Dan waved the morning newspaper across the kitchen table. "Have you read the latest on the corroded pipeline? Listen to this.

Environmentalists warn the oil leak at the refinery could have serious impact on marine life and seabird populations. Harbour clean-up is not expected to begin until—"

"Dan," said Karla, "I don't give a damn about oily seabirds or sick fish." She clinked their coffee mugs into the dishwasher, raked a straggle of hair behind an ear and turned to face him. Dan always dreaded that stance – his wife leaning back against the counter, arms crossed, eyes like two burned holes in a blanket. "What I do care about is your nursing degree. Explain to me how a nursing student can live one hour outside the city, the hospital, and the university. You ARE re-enrolling in third year, right? Don't even think about telling me otherwise."

"Yes, Karla. I'll finish, I'll finish." Dan's gaze moved to the open window, his thoughts drifting on the incoming breeze.

Maybe…

The dishwasher clunked and gurgled into action as Dan folded the newspaper and rose from the table. Karla continued her dispute from across the kitchen. "Look. Matt and I love it here in Port Sherman, okay?" she said, thrusting her palms to the ceiling. "The city life, our house—"

"But there you go again, Karla. It's not our house, is it? It was Ma's and Dad's and they've been dead two years. It's time to move out. Get a fresh start in our own place."

"Our own place. You keep babbling about that, but we lived in MY parents' basement for ten whole years. So, why the sudden need for our own place?"

"Well… that was different, wasn't it? Happier days. Matthew was little."

Matthew shook cereal into a bowl. "Yep," he said, "and now I'm big. Wow, who could have seen that coming?"

"Eat up," said Karla to the boy. "And grab your lunch there

on the counter."

Dan glanced at his watch. "Am I driving you this morning, Matt?"

"Not a chance. I'm takin' the bus," he replied. "I'd rather talk to the old lady who collects bird nests. No offence."

Dan gave it another shot as he backed through the living room to the front door. "Honey, just give it some thought. We could quite easily sell this place—"

"No, you give it some thought," she snapped. "We're not uprooting a thirteen-year-old kid to live in some... some hick town. Now, get to work. Pick up more rat traps."

Dan quietly closed the door behind him and trudged down his parents' old wheelchair ramp. Its rotting boards groaned beneath his tall and sturdy frame. He knew it needed to be pried off the front of the house, but Matthew's incessant howling about demolishing his skateboard ramp meant the crowbar would have to wait. With a weary grunt, Dan slumped into the driver's seat of his Ford sedan and grimaced through the windshield at the house and property. Even dandelions struggled to survive on the lawn – their wilted heads bent in the scraggy patches of turf and bedrock. Winnie-the-Pooh curtains still drooping in the window of Graeme's would-be nursery – a baby shrine untouched in a house of painful memories. He popped the car into reverse and, ignoring the gaggle of teenage girls smoking in the bus shelter, backed out onto the street.

It was often in slow morning traffic that Dan would contemplate the decision he had made three years before – when he'd put his nursing studies on hold to care for his parents, and moved his pregnant wife and ten-year-old, Matthew, into the family home. The living arrangement had certainly been comfortable enough. Not to mention rent-free. Setting up the two hospital beds in the living room had worked out extremely well, allowing Dan, Karla and Matthew full use of the rest of the house. And Matthew had always seemed happy – trouncing his grandfather at Crazy Eights every evening was all the entertainment he required. As for the old folk, they'd been content in their makeshift hospital room in the loving care of their son, watching their TV game shows, gazing through the picture window at the buses, the dog across the street, the clouds drifting by. Sure, his mother had been combative at times, but so had Karla. And yes, tensions had run high. But Dan felt confident he'd made all the right moves. No regrets. Not a single nagging doubt. However, the time had come, and Dan wanted out – an end to city smother, an end to Matthew's asthma attacks, to Karla's chronic melancholy and her morbid ties to the house. An end to lingering memories of oxygen tanks, bedpans and suffering in a place he no longer called home.

Back at the house, Matthew was in full-blown panic mode. Nothing unnerved him more than the notion of a new school, teenage drop-in centres, little white churches. Slinging his backpack over his shoulder, he turned to his mother. "You guys can't make me move!"

"Pfft! Don't mind your father," she said. "It's called mid-life crisis. It'll blow over. Next thing you know, he'll be wanting a nipple ring."

"But why Oyster Bay? This totally bites, Mom."

"You heard him, Matt. Fresh air and all that. Now get going." Matthew headed for the door.

"BYE!" Karla hollered. "GOT YOUR PUFFER?" but the slamming door and the squeaky brakes of the transit bus was all that was heard.

Dan inched his way toward the inner city. The once-elegant

MacEachern property, now home to six rental flats, stood stripped of its dignity beside the river. Having once marked the respected boundary where city ends and county begins, its forgiving property lines eventually fell victim to urban sprawl, leaving nothing but a few heritage photographs to attest to its glory days. Its magnificent front entrance, once gleaming of mahogany and bevelled glass, was now a wall of metal doors and rusty mail slots. Its gracious wrap-around veranda now cluttered with beer bottles, lawn chairs, motorcycle parts, and its apple orchard bulldozed to oblivion. As a child, Dan had often helped old man MacEachern pick the mushy windfalls from the orchard floor and drop them into his wife's outstretched apron. "For the cider," she'd smile, winking at the old man. Dan never understood the nuance, nor did he question it. The MacEachern orchard had been the most magical place on earth.

Nothing but a druggie house now. Nothing but a damned druggie house.

Fiddling with the air conditioning, Dan rolled up the windows. Exhaust fumes rose from the warm asphalt and bins of rotting compost littered the sidewalk. He turned onto the main thoroughfare where the orange-gray haze of the cityscape sprawled out before him. Port Sherman Harbour lay flat and motionless. Along its northern shore at the mouth of the estuary, all that remained of the pulp and paper mill was its condemned wastewater pond, still laden with hazardous waste, awaiting the Department of Environment's decision on sludge disposal. To the east, a jungle of steel pipes at the oil refinery stood hard against the morning sun. Plumes of noxious emissions billowed on the breeze as the stench of hydrogen sulfide settled over the city.

Nice. Business as usual at the Big Smoke. Never mind the oil leak.

Dazed at the traffic light, Dan recalled his conversation with his father on his last day at the refinery. "Asbestos sickness, son. You'll know the fancy name for it. I'm all tuckered out now, and I'm done."

"But, Dad, if you're sick, what about Ma? Who'll look after Ma?"

"Darned if I know, son. If my payout's good, I could maybe keep the day nurse for a while longer. But I can't see your ma through the nights any more. Can't do it. All such a shame, isn't it... hey, remember the day she danced across the kitchen after landing the dry cleaner job? Wasn't she excited? That was the start of it, wasn't it, son? Yep, and just look at her now."

Of course, Dan remembered that day. His mother had embarrassed the heck out of him. It was during the Christmas holidays, and she'd been arranging slices of stale fruit cake on a plate for him and Jessica Carr. To be fair, Jessica was way out of his league and, to be honest, the day had already deteriorated some. But it went straight to hell when his mother answered the phone, screamed "I GOT THE JOB!" and launched the fruit cake into the air. The plate came crashing first, followed by a heavy rain of blackened dates and raisins, and then she danced across the floor through the entire mess. "Practically in our own backyard, Danny! I won't even need a bus pass!" Oh yes, she was excited all right. Ecstatic. Over the proverbial moon. He never saw Jessica again.

Unfortunately, over the course of the following ten years, his mother's liver, kidneys and central nervous system had become severely damaged by the dry-cleaning solvent perchlorethylene, or PERC as the workers called it. Two other employees who lived nearby also fell victim to the solvent poisoning, and Dan's street became known as "PERC Alley", which was a constant source of humiliation for his parents.

Dan coasted slowly past the university campus, where the sixteen-storey medical research building shot skyward amid the old brick-and-mortar lecture halls. Hunkered within its chilly laboratories, Dan had spent countless hours hunched over the microscope, plunged deeply into his first-year research project, consumed by the causes and effects of neural toxicity. Its early signs. His mother's headaches, loss of memory, blurred vision. If only he'd recognized it earlier.

"Go back and get your degree, Danny," she had whispered from her bed. "Find that place in the country you always wanted… and take good care of little Matty. Always sick. And that wife of yours… no life, no energy, since losing the—"

"I will, Ma," he said, as he put the bent straw to her lips. "I will." But whether those promises would ever be kept would remain to be seen.

Dan pulled into the hospital parkade.

CHAPTER 2

"Mawning, Dan!" Jinghua shouted as she struggled to slide two heavy cardboard boxes from her passenger seat.

"Here, Jing, wait! I'll get those." Dan strode toward her.

"You carry faw me? Handouts faw ze meeting. New surgical guidelines… hey, why you look so stressout?"

"Oh, you know, always flogging the same dead horse," he sighed. "I mean, seriously, am I asking so much?" He jostled the boxes onto his shoulders. "Lots of people , right? I wanna hear crickets at night, not bloody sirens. You know? Maybe grow a few tomatoes."

"Siren? Don't cry to me about siren," she laughed. "I'm from Shanghai, don't fawget."

To the bemusement of her co-workers, Jinghua's accent would frequently spill out in her speech despite her best efforts to contain it. Straight bangs, black and glossy, grazed the rims of her thick spectacles and she would oftentimes fling her hair to the side with violent jerks of her head. This particular habit, along with her constant blinking, often irritated Dan… and her unbelievably tiny feet. "How can anyone's feet be that small, and what does the name Jinghua actually mean, anyway?" he had once asked, but her exhaustive narrative of the ancient origin of her name caused him never to ask again.

Together, they squeezed into the packed elevator as it rose to the eighth floor, and when the two stepped into their narrow corridor, Jinghua upped her pace to skip alongside him. Casual

Friday, a day for wearing shorts. Dan's female co-workers eagerly awaited their weekly gawk at his long legs, tanned and corded with muscles.

"Where do you want the boxes?" he asked, glancing around Jinghua's cramped cubicle.

"Just onna floor, thanks." She sat down and powered her computer.

Dan hesitated. "Jing?"

"Ya?"

"I'm in big trouble."

Jinghua fiddled noisily in a desk drawer. "Aw, c'mon now. Give it time. You soon sleep with ze crickets."

"No, not that."

Jinghua swiveled around in her office chair and tapped the cardboard boxes, motioning for him to sit.

Dan lowered himself to sit eye level with her. "It's school."

"Matthew skip school again?"

"No, no," said Dan.

"Black mold at the school again?"

"No, Jing! MY school! Nursing school. I can't get back in. Been out too long." Dan blew out a long breath. "See, I didn't complete second year, but Karla thinks I did. Then I took two consecutive one-year leaves, which essentially adds up to three years absent."

"Wait, wait. You only finish first yeeaw?"

"Pretty much," he sighed.

"You have to start all over?"

"Yep, I've been pleading with the Registrar for weeks, but the ruling is clear. I need to fully reapply to the Bachelor of Nursing program starting in first year. Karla thinks this office job here is just temporary. She thinks I'm re-enrolling in third year in the fall."

"Ohhhh. What you gonna do?"

"Well, I don't mind saying, I do like this job, and the steady paycheck sure as hell takes the sting out of my academic predicament. No clue how to break it to Karla, though. Think I'll just ride it out some more." Dan groaned and pushed himself to his feet.

Jinghua blinked a few times, folded her arms and leaned back in her chair. "Confucius say—"

"Don't even go there!" Dan held up a hand. "No ancient proverb's gonna help me now. It ain't gonna be pretty, Jing. Karla's gonna tear me limb from limb."

Jinghua turned back to her computer screen. "Hmm. Good zing you have doctor friends," she said.

Dan plopped down at his desk and ran his fingers through his long, loose curls. Oblivious to admiring glances, he fixed his porcelain-blue eyes to the screen and waited for his computer to boot. His co-workers knew he was stressed. The signs were all there – the muscles flexing in his square jaw, the thrumming of his fingertips on his coffee mug.

The hospital logo whirled in three colourful loops before stopping mid screen:

PORT SHERMAN HEALTH AUTHORITY
Achieving Better Health Care
One Patient at a Time

Dan Duggan worked in Operating Room bookings where every morning on his arrival there was – what he called – a "brushfire" burning. Dan's job was to stabilize the situation and keep as many elective surgeries as possible on schedule. A surgeon may have fallen sick, the orthopedic waitlist may have grown overnight, or a scheduling error may have caused a nursing shortage in Recovery Room. The blaze burning on this particular morning was in the Emergency Department. Overnight, they had listed eleven patients for immediate surgery, leaving Dan to rearrange the day's schedule. "What the heck happened down there last night?" he asked the night nurse coming off duty.

"Oh, you know, let's see, a spinal fracture, an appendix, a strangulated hernia, a couple gallbladders. Work your magic, Dan. I'm goin' home."

Highly skilled in troubleshooting and mediation, Dan worked proficiently with surgeons, anesthesiologists, nurses, and technicians alike. After several hours of phones ringing, e-mails dinging, pagers beeping and tempers flaring, Dan accommodated all eleven emergency patients without canceling a single elective surgery. The Chief of Obstetrics stood behind him in the cafeteria line. "Dan Duggan, you continue to amaze us. You're a juggler, puppeteer, and snake charmer rolled into one," he chuckled.

"Heh heh, you think so?" said Dan. "Because none of those powers seem to work with the wife." He should have used her name, he knew. But mere mention of the name, Karla, could possibly cause this silver-haired, crinkly-eyed Whisperer of Unborn Babies to make the Duggan name connection, and suddenly recall that awful night in Emergency, before Dan joined the hospital staff.

There'd been not a twitch from the baby in twenty-four hours, and Karla lay belly-up on the stretcher. The obstetrician had tucked away his fetal stethoscope and patted her hand. "Let's take a ride up to ultrasound, shall we? Take a closer look." An hour later, when the dreaded news was confirmed, Dan had watched dumbstruck as the doctor scrolled through Karla's online chart. "Thirty-five weeks gestation, normal fetal development... no issues or concerns in prenatal history. One previous, healthy delivery ten years ago?"

"Yes, our son, Matthew."

"Mr. Duggan, did your wife use alcohol or any drugs, prescription or otherwise, during her pregnancy?"

"No. Just iron pills."

"Has she suffered an injury, or had an accident of any kind?"

"No."

"Would you say she's been under any amount of stress?"

And there it was. The low rumble of thunder.

"Ah... yes. I guess you could say that. We take care of my parents. They're both quite ill and require a lot of care."

Karla sobbed quietly on the other side of the drape.

"So, she overdid it with lifting and such? Lack of rest?"

Guilt wormed its way up his throat. "Emotional stress," he said, dropping his eyes to the floor. "My mother... she's always been unkind toward Karla, but these last few months, well, she's been downright nasty." Dan's voice broke as he met the doctor's gaze. "B-but my mom's terminally ill, and she's bedridden, and I just overlooked it. I turned a blind eye." Dan dropped his elbows to his knees and hid his face in his hands.

"Okay. Be with her now," the doctor had said, nodding toward the drape. "We'll keep her overnight and likely induce labour, maybe do some testing to try and find an explanation, but studies have shown moms with high levels of psychological stress have a greater risk of miscarriage than those with moderate stress levels." He touched Dan's arm. "Most unfortunate, Mr. Duggan, but these things do happen." Dan sat stunned as the doctor disappeared from view, then he swished open the drape, collapsed across Karla's heaving chest, buried his face in the crook of her neck and wept.

"It's not your fault, Danny," Karla had said. "Not your fault."

Three years since that fateful night, and the sight of that obstetrician never failed to kick open the floodgates of guilt and regret. Now, robbed of all appetite, Dan found an empty table along the back wall of the cafeteria, slid a piece of cold pizza across a paper plate, and thumbed through his tattered copy of *Day Sailing. A Beginner Guide.*

CHAPTER 3

An aerial view of Oyster Bay portrays a strawberry-shaped body of tranquil waters tucked safely into Nova Scotia's jagged coastline. Taking refuge from the turbulent ocean, the aqua of its sandy shallows deepens to an indigo blue. Along its southern shoreline, wharves jut out like matchsticks from the clusters of warehouses at the waterfront. Known as "Town Centre", its streets reach uphill from the bustling main artery, Bayshore Drive, into a cross-hatching of leafy neighbourhoods overlooking the bay.

As the bay's shoreline sweeps inland, a luxurious golf course separates Town Centre from its western community. Dimpled with bunkers, its velvety greens extend to the overhang at water's edge. At the marina, white specks of fiberglass vessels glisten at their moorings. Clusters of rooftops dot the hillsides, peeking through the lush green canopy on Austin Road, as it winds around its western shore. The residents of this community known as "Westside" like to think they live on the moneyed side of town.

Oyster Bay's Town Centre bears small resemblance to its earlier years, when its lifeblood was the sea. Before it was demolished, the fish processing plant had been the central core of the town. For decades, fishing trawlers had dumped their lucrative catches into the rough and reddened hands of the assembly line workers, lining the pockets and filling the hungry bellies of its townspeople. A certain pride and camaraderie had existed between the plant workers and those who toiled on the sea, and the town had enjoyed a stable and steady economy. The eventual collapse of the inshore cod fishery, however, brought those days to a grinding halt, causing the widespread departure of much of Oyster Bay's workforce.

For a time, the town managed to remain afloat on the dollars of the affluent – elite golfers, sailing enthusiasts and sport fishermen. But not until sparkling tourism ads and government initiatives attracted artisans and entrepreneurs to the area, did the town begin to repopulate. The waterfront was entirely refurbished with new wharves, warehouses, and colourful shops and restaurants, breathing new hope into the hearts of those who managed to hang onto their homes and survive the scrape. But, sadly, not everyone bounced back. Those who lost everything rely on government assistance, and continue to gather in ragged groups around town, taking over the tourist benches and generally spoiling the ambience. NO LOITERING signs installed throughout the town are mostly disregarded, forcing a few frustrated shop owners to remove planter boxes and other comfy sitting surfaces outside their doors. The unsightly panhandlers however, like living chess pieces, simply shift from one location to another. Stories of a food bank opening in town keep them sniffing around for tidbits of information, and a group sits in daily vigil under the enormous red maple, across from the only vacant retail property on Bayshore Drive. "Gotta be the place," they say, spitting bits of tobacco. "This here's gonna be the food bank." But another day passes, then another and, as each day ends, they trudge hungry and disheartened back to the outskirts of town.

***

Dan dropped two loonies in the parking meter, grabbed an espresso, found a bench on the government wharf, and spread the Oyster Bay real estate flyer across his knees. Karla would never know. He'd take a quick peek at a few properties. A walk about town. Get a feel for the place, that's all. He pried the plastic lid from his espresso. Purple jellyfish pulsated in the waters of the shallows, tangling their tentacles in the broken remains of the massive posts that once supported the fish plant. Dan recalled its faded green shingles, its windows buzzing with flies. Strolling the wharf with his parents on their Sunday outings. The smell of creosote planks baking in the sun. Old Oyster Bay, where a slippery fresh cod with eyes clear as glass could be purchased from an ice-filled tub on the tailgate of a truck. A cod with a clouded eye, of course, was yesterday's catch.

Rolling the flyer into a stiff tube, Dan slapped it against his palm, pushed himself to his feet and ventured down Bayshore Drive. Along the sidewalk, he paused to run his fingertips along a massive oak plank – the words "Building on Tradition" chiseled deeply into its fibers. Ah yes. The new wooden boat-building school, offering an apprentice program like no other, with a student waiting list a mile long. A completed project in the form of a 16-foot fishing dory sat behind the sign on the lawn. Dan peered up the walkway to the entrance.

Matthew might someday take an interest in something like this. I wonder if they have a brochure... no. Stay the course. Keep walking.

Dan headed uphill into the surrounding neighbourhoods and lost all track of time. Only when his stomach began to growl did he check his watch. Precisely how many coins he had dropped into the parking meter was now lost from memory. An Oyster Bay parking ticket would not be good. Karla would get to the bottom of that.

Dan had easily located and eyeballed the four properties in the flyer and, although they were only curbside assessments, he felt the stirrings of new beginnings. All were tidy, well-kept working-class homes with simple charm and character. Homes that spoke of homegrown pride, with colourful garden sheds, sunporches, and mature trees. He stopped to take a breather on the worn concrete steps of the landmark Ocean Academy. According to what he'd heard on the news, its long-deserted classrooms would be alive and bustling again in September with the start-up of two diploma programs – Culinary Arts, and Aesthetic Therapies – and according to the chatty fellow raking the lawn, this was just the beginning. "Oh yah, lots more courses coming," he said leaning on his rake.

Dan took in the sweeping view. "Beautiful neighbourhood," he said. "You live up here?"

"Down there," he pointed. "Next door to the hospital. I look after their lawns too."

Dan watched an ambulance pull away from its doors. His elective in Community Medicine spent there at Horizon Community Hospital, would remain his most cherished memory of nursing school. How he'd love to stop in to see the new blood collection laboratory and renal dialysis unit… not to mention the updated Emergency Department, newly equipped to handle Level Two Emergencies.

"You on foot? Because I got water, if you—"

"Oh, no thanks," said Dan. He stood and stretched. "My car's down the waterfront just begging for a parking ticket."

Famished, Dan hurried downhill, arrived at Bayshore Drive and waited at the crosswalk. Poking impatiently at the pedestrian light, he tried to ignore the aroma of fresh coffee and cinnamon rolls wafting along the sidewalk. "C'mon, c'mon," he grumbled, squinting at the crosswalk light. Suddenly – and like a jab in an empty stomach – a woman's voice. "Hello there! Won't you join us?"

The pedestrian light turned green. Dan hesitated.

"Over here!" she called out.

Dan turned toward the voice. "Me?" he asked.

"Art and Heritage Days," said the woman. "Right here at Town Hall," she gestured toward its open double doors. Dan peered across the road toward his vehicle and jerked a thumb in its direction. "Parking meter!"

"You must be from out of town. There's no parking fee on weekends!"

Planting his palm to his forehead, Dan laughed. "Oyster Bay owes me some serious coin, then!"

The woman approached him with a handful of pamphlets. "Hi, I'm Mayor Romans. Feel free to browse our art exhibits, every Sunday at eleven, until Labour Day," she said. "Paintings, pottery, sculpture. All local talent. Donation box is just inside the door. Any small contribution is appreciated." Dan took a pamphlet as the she swept her silk scarf over a shoulder. "That is, if you have any spare change left," she laughed.

Dan passed through Town Hall's massive oak doors to a noisy and colourful crowd of art enthusiasts and Sunday morning market goers. Oyster Bay's academics and creative thinkers, peering intently at brushstrokes and clay forms, in their socks and sandals, man-buns and beards, free-flowing skirts and granny glasses – and blocking the damned refreshments table. Dan kept his eyes to the floor, and managed a hasty browse throughout the exhibits and then, after a cold coffee and stale roll, headed across Bayshore Drive to his car. No texts from Karla. Good. Still at church with her parents. She'll be none the wiser. He stuffed the "Art and Heritage" pamphlet in a trash bin, but the real estate flyer... well, he'd have to keep that a while. The advertisement alone had won him over:

Known for its ocean cuisine, yachting events, music festivals and whale watching, Oyster Bay offers up a seaside home, fresh and vibrant, scenic and chic, steeped in the stories of seafarers. All within an hour's drive of Port Sherman.

CHAPTER 4

In the cramped and cluttered vestry of the Church of the Holy Trinity in Westside Oyster Bay, the Reverend Terrence Fry, or The "Friar" as he liked to be called, busied himself with the new choir robes. Sorting by size, he slipped them onto hangers and, with a theatrical sweep of his arm, slid the shimmering robes of royal blue across the rack.

Jolly good work! Keep those donations rolling in!

Reverend Fry had been in office for nine years and had seen the church through countless upgrades. As with most parishes, membership had fallen off in recent years, but still, he managed to raise substantial funds whenever necessary. Simply by request, a Service of Baptism or Holy Matrimony would be offered to anyone – complete strangers to the church – if willing to pay the hefty fee. "I turn nobody away," he would sing in his own defence but, in the Parish Council, many eyebrows were raised at that remark, for he most certainly did turn his back on parishioners with little to offer the collection plate.

The Church of the Holy Trinity had had a bumpy time with priests. In the three years preceding Reverend Fry, there had been two incumbents – a female, faint-hearted and mousy, who lacked the grit and back-slapping character to appease the old boys, and a male, newly ordained and acne-scarred, with enough fanatical fervour to drive even the most dispassionate members home to their liquor cabinets, never to return. Therefore, despite being a bit of an odd duck and rather unorthodox in his views, the

Reverend Terrence Fry, with his British roots and flamboyant personality, was deemed the perfect fit. So keen was the bishop to accommodate his needs, he cast tradition to the wind and granted Reverend Fry permission to forego living in the church rectory, to lead a more private life in his own apartment across town. With this condition met, the Friar took up office.

A colourful preacher with a love for attention and an edge for drama, Reverend Fry had no trouble filling the pews each Sunday. He would, however, without hesitation, dismiss anyone with an annoying cough or disruptive child. In fact, one memorable morning, feeling robbed of the spotlight by a handsome seeing-eye dog, he hustled both dog and master out the door. This was, some would say, his first faux pas.

Reverend Fry's honesty and integrity began to come under scrutiny within his first year in office, sparking the Diocese to delve into his spending practices. His first reprimand awaited him on return from an unauthorized trip to his homeland, and his travel was curtailed indefinitely. Then, like fanned flames, suspicions of bribery and political patronage also began sweeping throughout the parish. Tales of unrecorded donations and tax fraud caused the diocese to order full financial audits of the accounts, but the Friar's books always came up clean. Even after the infamous group of church custodians dared to file a police report accused him of stealing church property, his reputation remained unscathed. His devoted followers simply dismissed all rumours and credited him with keeping the church in fine repair and meeting the spiritual needs of his flock. His accusers, however, were eternally shunned from church and community.

***

When the choir robes were all accounted for, the Friar gently lifted his own new vestments from the shipping crate and traced a pudgy finger around the delicate, silk embroidered images – the Dove and Olive Branch, the Crucifix, the Tree of Life. Lifting each garment to his face, he breathed in their satiny folds.

Expensive, oh yes. But exquisite.

Clutching each one to his chest, and preening himself in the full-length mirror, the eyes of the fearful young lad from Lancashire gazed back at him. Despite the Friar's best efforts to turn away, those eyes would always hold him captive. The haunting, hazel eyes of young Terrence. Always beseeching. How could Mother not know? Even the wretched tourists seemed to know something. Oh, how he detested them – their clumsy tumble from the tour bus, consulting their maps, then spreading out in all directions in front of the tiny stone cottage in which he lived. And they'd return from their walking tours and shopping trips and, while waiting for their bus to return, would congregate around his front garden, bloody-well obsessed with the upstairs window. "Up there in the peak, see?" they'd say. "How quaint. All those tiny panes. The glass appears original, as well. It can't be someone's bedroom, though. Must be an attic. The house has to be, what, sixteenth century? Imagine the narrow staircase in that place."

Young Terrence had incessantly questioned the logic behind the tour bus stopping precisely there on his doorstep. After all, the medieval pub was over the bridge on the far side of the river, the castle ruins around the corner and up the hill, and all the teacup and trinket shops farther down the road. So why not STOP further down the road? His parents weren't bothered by the bus stop though. Not in the least. In fact, they rather enjoyed the odd chat with the tourists and would even pose for photos in the garden, as the driver hopped down to curbside for a smoke – engine roaring, spewing black exhaust into the air. Terrence would avoid any such encounter like the plague and skitter in his short pants and knee socks through the narrow alleyway to his back door. Out front though, the loud and obnoxious voices would persist. "Stand right there, darlin'. Right in front of them red flowers. Hold it now, I need to back up. Gotta get that upstairs window in."

The tiny eight-paned window at the centre of everyone's storybook imaginations was indeed in a bedroom – Terrence's bedroom – and in those years of his childhood, he suffered a twisting anxiety that one day a nosey tourist would break down the door, tiptoe up the bending staircase, and view the other side of the enchanted window – where they'd witness the pungent odour of unwashed clothes and tangled bed linens. A pigsty of chaos and disorder. Where dubious acts of fatherly love were consummated, and where the romance of the English nursery rhyme would surely die a sudden death.

***

Jolted from his reverie in front of the mirror, and suddenly aware of the time, the Friar swiftly snapped into action and donned his robe for the funeral of the late Archie MacLeod. Looking exceedingly holy in his purple satin, the Friar cast a worried glance into the church, ducked back into the vestry, and rummaged through the cupboards.

Now, where's an empty box. A box, a box. I need a decent-sized box.

Good old Archie had packed the quaint, country church and

outside in the cemetery, an unseasonably cold Atlantic fog drifted up from the water, settling like a wet blanket over the village of Westside Oyster Bay. Mourners huddled together at his gravesite, white vapours of breath escaping their lips, as Archie's marble urn descended into its resting place. When the crowd began to disperse, Alice MacLeod took a few moments to kneel alone at her late husband's grave. Desiree, her daughter, stood a distance away, lifting her coat collar to the dampness. "Please Archie, I hope you can find it in your heart to forgive me," said the widow. She then struggled to a standing position, slipped her arm into her daughter's, and ascended the hill to the parking lot. Reverend Fry had already returned to the warmth of the church.

"I'll be but a minute, Desiree," Alice said, as she stepped quickly into the vestry, and pressed a thick envelope into the Friar's hand. In return, he passed Alice a cardboard box which read: "Theodore Christian Products – Communion Wafers – Box of 1000."

CHAPTER 5

The travel trailer was stifling and stuffy with cigarette smoke as the morning sun burned into its metal roof. Someone was beating on the door. "Rent! I've come for the rent!" shouted the voice outside. The old retriever struggled to stand as Willy opened the door.

"First month up already? Juss a minute," he said. He rummaged for the tobacco tin stashed in a compartment over the sink and clawed open its lid. Fumbling with the bills, he counted them aloud. "It's all there," he said, as he handed over the cash.

"This here's only forty-five," said the property owner. "Thought we settled on fifty."

"Ahh, no. You said forty-five since I can't use the well water."

"Oh. Right," he snapped, his gaze shifting to the shattered well crocks sitting half hidden in the alders. "Rain barrel holding out?"

"Yup," he nodded. "I boil it before drinkin'."

"Keeping the dog quiet, like I said?"

"Yup," he said, dropping his hand to her uplifted snout.

"Good, because folks here in Westside don't take kindly to strangers, 'specially noisy ones," he said. He folded the cash into his wallet, then picked his way through a tangle of thorny bushes and unkept lilacs, back to his stately home, pristine property and manicured lawns. Willy stepped outside the trailer and tossed his bread crusts to the crows. "Now, Gert, you leave that alone," he said to the dog. "I'll get yer breakfast in a bit."

Back inside, as he squeezed through the passageway to the dogfood cupboard, the tattered photograph that had been propped on a shelf fluttered to the floor. Coughing and groaning, he bent to pick it up. Gert stopped abruptly behind him, eyes fixed on the dogfood cupboard. Now completely distracted, Willy dropped into his chair as a cloud of dog hair floated up in the slanted rays of the sun. The dog landed in a heap at his feet, for she knew this scenario well. Her master would sit now, and stare at that photo, and forget all about her, and her breakfast, and whatever else he was doing at the time. She raised an eyebrow to watch as he rubbed his two thumbs along its tattered edges. An ear twitched at the crowing in the trees outside and, with stomach growling, Gert gently rested her chin on his bare foot and waited it out.

The photograph was taken on his fifteenth birthday. Willy would never forget his parents' excitement over the new fishing rod – how he awoke to their giggling as they tried sneaking it into his room. "Happy Birthday, son," his father had said. "Rise and shine! High tide is at one. Mom packed us a lunch. Let's go catch us some mackerel!" Still vivid in his memory was the sulphuric smell of egg salad sandwiches, the burned bottoms of the peanut butter cookies, the salty Boston fog on the government wharf, his father's warm hands on his. "You gotta reel it in steady like this," his dad had said. "Oh, now that's a beauty, right there! Nice catch, son! Nice catch!"

"HOLD IT UP!" his mother hollered, fumbling for her camera, just as the black lady walked by.

"Here, ma'am. Let me take that picture for you," said the lady. "All three of you."

"Would you? That's so kind!" His mother handed over the camera and scurried to join her grinning husband and son.

"Y'all smile now," the lady laughed, and CLICK. That moment, now frozen in time, marked the end of the only family life Willy ever knew. He often wondered if the black lady knew what was about to happen. How could she not have noticed the loop of bright yellow rope lying on the wharf? How could she not have noticed that it encircled his mother's ankles and could suddenly spring to life like a snake. His mind, still swollen with images, plays the nightmare over and over. His mother violently snatched from the wharf and flung into the churning wake of the tuna boat. Her red sweater a murky shadow under the surface. His father's blood-curdling screams for help. Leaping up and down on the wharf, arms flailing. "STOP! STOP!" His sudden plunge into the harbour. Furiously swimming, clawing and slapping at the water, waving and hollering, swimming farther and farther out, until the tiny speck of his head sank below the surface, and the tuna boat disappeared around the point.

Willy tries hard to remember that blurry interval that followed, when his senses seemed to short circuit and all went quiet. But then, like a flickering home movie, the reel rolls again and the black lady's warm arms are holding him tightly, and she's kneeling on the rough planks in her shiny nylon stockings. "Shh, child," she whispers. "Shh, now." She smelled so nice, soft like powder. Back and forth she rocked him, both of them collapsed on the wharf. The mackerel lay still and gaping. A policeman kicked it over the side. PLOP. Why did an ambulance come? His parents were underwater. More sirens and a rescue boat. Going in the wrong direction. Dad didn't swim that way… he swam that other way…

***

The dog waited patiently at his feet. "C'mon Gert, I'll feed ya now," he sighed. "We'll lay low again today. You heard what the fella said. The likes of us aren't welcome around these parts."

CHAPTER 6

The glowing strip of orange on the horizon of the Atlantic would not illuminate Westside Oyster Bay for another hour, but Alice MacLeod's eyes suddenly shot open. Lying on her side with her knees drawn up, she stared into the darkness – that deep blackness that lies just beyond the light of the clock.

Perfect! That's exactly what I'll use. Just the right size.

She couldn't wait to get started. It was 4.44 a.m. and she was giddy with excitement. With a squirm in her belly, she rolled over and wondered how it came to her.

No one will ever know. Not Desiree. Not even Sully.

Alice writhed and wiggled until daylight, then flung off her blankets like a child on Christmas morning. Shivering in her nightgown, she rushed down the flight of stairs to the workshop. The sunrise streaming through the basement window had crept its way across the floor when Alice's bare feet came to a stop. There it was. Sitting among the clutter of unfinished projects and objects to be repaired. Alice lifted it, along with its broken-off piece, from the pile. Blowing away a layer of dust, she began to hatch her plan. She placed both pieces on the workbench and plugged the glue gun into the electrical socket. Exhilarated, Alice climbed the basement stairs and boiled the kettle.

First, a cup of tea. Teabags, teabags, here they are. Now... oh, and I mustn't forget this.

Alice snatched a container from the counter and clutched it to her chest. With hot tea slopping, she scurried back to the workshop. Warm white globules dripped from the glue gun.

Better check the doors.

Up the stairs she clambered again, checked the locks and skittered back to the basement. Alice took a deep breath and collapsed onto the worn, wooden stool. Suspended dust mites in the morning sun drifted about her frail figure, her thin gray hair lay flattened from a fitful sleep. She took a gulp of scalding tea and sputtered. Her eyes lingered on the rack of deer antlers displayed over the workshop door, the handsaws lined up along the wall, and Archie's beloved old yardsticks.

Had I allowed it, he would have collected everything known to man.

Alice tapped the birdseed residue from the large metal funnel and placed it on the workbench. She looked one way, then she looked the other, her mind racing. From a dusty overhead shelf, she lifted down the bulky electric drill – the 'heavy old clunker', Archie used to call it. Fumbling through the drill bits, Alice felt dizzy and detached. Staring dumbly at the scattering of grimy metal bits, her arthritic fingers plucked out the largest bit and locked it into the drill chuck. She then shuffled along the bench to the vise.

The most useful tool in the workshop is the vise. Archie always said.

Placing her project in its jaws, she tightened its clamp until it took a firm hold.

Heaven forbid if I crack this thing.

Positioning the drill bit in the critical location and, careful not to apply too much pressure, the old girl painstakingly drilled down until the bit plunged into the empty space. Sighing with relief, she poked her baby finger through the hole and ran it around the smooth inside surface. She then reached for the container she had snatched from the kitchen and, placing the funnel into the hole, poured the substance through. A few moments later, when her trembling subsided, she hot glued the broken piece in place, concealing the drilled hole, closing the vessel, and hiding her wrongdoing.

ONE YEAR LATER

CHAPTER 7

The weathered Cape Cod house at 131 Pinehill Avenue, Town Centre Oyster Bay, sat nestled in a stand of Eastern white pines as crate after crate tumbled off the moving van. Its location was ideal – a two-minute walk uphill from the waterfront shops. Karla climbed the staircase to Matthew's bedroom dragging yet another box of cables and speakers. The Scotch tape was yowling in protest as she entered the room.

"Tell me again why we moved here, Mom! I hate this place," he growled. The tape wouldn't hold his posters to the brittle wallpaper, he kept cracking his head on the ceiling, and there was only one electrical outlet in the entire room. His window in the tiny dormer "overlooked the backyard, where the driveway curved in from their mailbox on Pinehill Avenue. The front of the house, however, faced a side street, Jeffries Lane.". "How come I can't even stand up by my window over there?"

"That's all part of the charm," explained Karla. "You see, originally, these old Cape Cod houses had no dormers at all, maybe a window at each end, and the whole family would sleep up here. Then, to add more light, some homeowners would later add dormers, but they would be only high enough for a child to stand in."

"Friggin' lame," he muttered.

"Ready to check out the school?"

"You mean the one for babies? The so-called high school with grade sevens!" he yelped.

"That's the one," she said. "You're enrolled now. Let's go."

Matthew slung the roll of Scotch tape across the bed. "Okay, okay. I'm coming already."

Karla stopped abruptly in the doorway as they were leaving his room. "What's that stink in here?" she asked.

He pointed to his dresser. "Probably the dirty dishes over there. Old pizza or something."

"How in God's name did you manage to dirty the dishes already? We're hardly moved in!"

The boy shrugged. "They came from home. You told me to pack up my room."

"Hand them over," she growled. "Now!"

Later that day, when Dan asked about the school visit, Karla informed him that their son would rather serve time inside a maximum-security prison than within the walls of Captain J. Keller Consolidated School.

***

The boxes and bags were eventually unpacked and furniture arranged, and young Matthew settled into the unusual dwelling where the warmth of the sun bathed the private backyard each afternoon. Matthew was fascinated with the crooked back porch that smelled of warm wood and rubber boots. With the curiosity of a small child, he would open the wooden shutters to the clothesline, and shut them. Open them. Shut them.

"How come you use a clothesline, Mom? We got a dryer in the basement."

"Oh, you know, when in Rome."

"Huh?"

"I'm a country girl now. I'm supposed to hang out clothes!"

she laughed. "The love of a clothesline is a woman thing… you know, like making pickles."

"Did you ever make pickles?"

"In your father's dreams, maybe" she said.

The boy was equally obsessed with the pantry. "So, Dad says they rolled out pie dough in here, and made cookies and stuff. Hey, did you know these wooden things pull out to make more counter space? How come this cupboard down here is so drafty? Holy crap, I can see daylight through here. Look!"

Karla came to investigate. "Must have been a cold storage cupboard, you know, for root vegetables and such. We'll have to close that up somehow."

How Matthew longed to be eight years old again. What a cool place to hide with a Nerf gun. The enemy creeping up outside would never suspect a soldier crouched in there. Closing the door to the cupboard, he ventured again. "Think you'll ever make pies in here?"

"Give me a break!" Karla cried. "We just moved in. Pity's sake!"

The house was broken into undersized rooms which only added to its appeal. One step up from the back porch was the eat-in kitchen where creaky pine floorboards had shrunken over time and the brooms of a thousand sweepings had simply filled the cracks with dirt. A set of old metal cupboards lined one wall, and beneath lay a chipped countertop with a drain board sloping to an enamel sink. The brass faucets were charming and original but terribly inefficient, so Karla announced they would be the first upgrade.

If its leaf was removed, and the kitchen table was shoved tightly up against the wall, two people could enjoy a meal in comfort. But a meal for three required much bumping and rearranging of chairs, enabling the person sitting closest to the refrigerator to open its door while seated. The doorway from kitchen to living room was too low for Dan, causing him to duck his head when passing through, and Karla was beginning to fret about how much taller Matthew would become.

Two large windows with a door in the centre marked the front of the house which overlooked their sloped lawn and walkway down to Jeffries lane. A steep, narrow staircase running directly up from the front door divided the front of the house into two areas – one being the living room, the other serving as Karla's office. A brick fireplace stood at one end of the living room, and it was here that Dan and Karla had begun to relax in the evenings with their gardening books and magazines – the hushed and gentle sounds of their neighbourhood drifting through the open windows.

Karla's office overlooked a patch of gnarled rhododendrons which spread beneath her window on the front lawn and consisted of a desk, computer, printer, telephone, and a bookcase of binders. Dan had been right about everything, she thought. "You're a telephone surveyor, Karla," he had said. "You can work from any location. Think about that. You won't even miss the city!" Now, shameful of the fact that Matthew had to suffer a life-threatening asthma attack before she had come to her senses, Karla vowed to embrace their new life. She stepped back and tilted her head to admire her collection of Harlequin Romances stacked snuggly in a floor-to-ceiling cubby hole in the wall which was, in her best guess, a delightful and convenient building flaw. Dan tiptoed up behind her and slipped his arms around her waist. "See?" he whispered in her ear. "The house was built just for you and your Harlies."

Not wishing to concede victory further, she said, "I'm going up now, you coming?"

"Yawpp… I'm tired too," he yawned, and followed her up the staircase. A week of shuffling furniture and dragging boxes had left Dan ready to return to the office brushfires.

***

Jinghua stood at the copy machine. "Hey Danno! How was your first commute?"

"Beautiful! Fifty-five minutes, and so worth the drive," Dan beamed, lifting her off the floor in a bear hug. The other girls watched with envy as he flashed his radioactive smile around the office.

"When's the housewarming?" one laughed.

"Yah, Dan! Get your sailboat yet?"

Dan dropped Jinghua to the floor. "Patience ladies, patience! We're still trying to find space for everything!" Unbeknownst to Dan Duggan, finding space in the house would be the absolute least of his problems.

CHAPTER 8

Although widowed for a year, Alice existed in perfect peace in the sprawling, ranch-style bungalow where she and Archie had lived. Openly chattering to herself throughout the day, she often held down both sides of a conversation. Living in Westside Oyster Bay had been a great source of contentment for her. Snuggled up next door to the Church of The Holy Trinity, she not only served on the Women's Auxiliary and Sanctuary Guild but was recently appointed the esteemed office of Treasurer.

Standing in her backyard, Alice now wished she had taken photographs of the house over the years, as it had been renovated so many times. Her eyes moved along the cracked foundation and up the silvery shingles.

Let's see now, Desiree was still in her crib. Yes, that's right… then the new bathroom. Yes, and the kitchen reno came next.

Her gaze moved to the lace curtains in the kitchen window. Archie never understood the need for curtains. To him, they were simply view-blockers. Here at the back of the house the full foundation was exposed, affording a bright and sunny workshop. Archie had spent endless hours at his workbench overlooking the bay, so when Alice had suggested attaching her small greenhouse to the basement door, he was less than enthusiastic. "But I could access it from the workshop, Archie, and not have to walk across the yard, like on rainy days," she had pleaded. As always, Archie was eventually persuaded, and the greenhouse was installed at the basement door. Thereafter, they spent their days pursuing their hobbies elbow-to-elbow and over time their interests merged. Archie might spend a day planting seeds with Alice, or she might try her hand at a woodworking project.

She recalled one autumn afternoon when Archie was oiling his shotgun. "You'll hunt anything from sky, land or sea, won't you, Archie?" she had asked. "Why is it, I wonder? Why is deer hunting called hunting, and bird hunting called hunting, but fish hunting is called fishing?" Archie had put down his oil rag, and stared quizzically at his wife, unable to form an intelligent response.

Alice wandered along to her stone garden bench. The windchimes in the apple tree tinkled in the breeze as she seated herself on the cold stone slab. Those bothersome dizzy spells had kept her indoors throughout much of the early spring, but now she watched with high hopes as the clouds cleared out inch by inch across the sky. Her gardens had sprung to life in the warm rains and the lawns that swept down to the shore were yellow with dandelions. Not a single tree blocked her view of the Bay. Archie had seen to that. Town Centre was darkening across the water – its wharves and bulky warehouses receding into the shadows of the surrounding hillsides, and the wake of the evening whale-watching boat a thin white line.

Alice loved this time of evening, when the bay went still, the birds went silent, and everything in her house tucked in for the night. Her gaze hovered over the currant bushes, dropped to the mouth of the bay and across the open sea. Alice stared, lost in thought, her lifelong desire to see that distant shore still burning in her bosom. She had often annoyed Archie with her ramblings and endless questions. "The coast of France, yes, Archie, I know, but what exactly? Straight across the ocean from here, what do you suppose we'd see? A beach, a seaside village, a field of sheep, a vineyard?" Alice pulled a rumpled tissue from her shirtsleeve.

If only I'd learned the internet like Desiree wanted, I would have my answer. I could see it on that space camera. Ah, you old fool. It's too late now.

With a painful click of her knee, Alice rose from the bench, turned to the house and, pinching a dead geranium on her way through the greenhouse, headed upstairs. It was in the wee hours of the morning, under her patchwork quilt, alone with her clouded conscience, that Alice drew her last breath.

CHAPTER 9

Having made an early start from her apartment in downtown Port Sherman, Desiree MacLeod sped her compact SUV along Route 314 west into farm country. Her most trusted and valued business partners – the vegetable farmers of the lush and fertile Landsoe Valley – were always pleased to see her. Her annual visit to the sprawling green fields had become a tradition in the past few years, one that Desiree especially cherished. The holiday was still months away, but she had already received over two hundred requests for Christmas assistance. She smiled in anticipation of seeing the farmers' weathered faces again and hoped that this year's successful planting season would result in yet another bumper crop. Her phone vibrated on the passenger seat and, against her better judgement, she took the call while driving.

"Hey, Sully, what's up?"

She eased off on the accelerator. "What? No, listen to me," she said. "You need to calm down, okay?" Desiree stood on the brake, fish-tailing the vehicle to a stop on the shoulder, spitting dust and gravel into the air.

"I'm so sorry, Desiree!" Sully wailed. "I just dropped over with your mother's mail. I know where she hides her key. Her knee's been sore... I called out, but no answer. It was nine. She should have been up. I was gonna leave the mail on the table, but, but..."

"Sully! Settle down and tell me what's wrong!" Desiree's mouth had gone powder dry.

"Okay, I went down the hall to her room," she said, "and there she was, still in bed. I thought maybe she was sick, so I-I..." Her voice trailed off as she blew her nose.

"SULLY!"

"I knew she was dead," she sniffled. "I didn't feel for a pulse or nothing. She was so still and peaceful, and-and... like there was nothing wrong in the room. Her blankets were smooth and all like that."

Desiree gripped the wheel. "No. You're mistaken. Okay? Call 911. Call them right NOW. I'm turning around. I'll be there in a couple of hours. I'm way out in Landsoe!"

"I won't let anyone take her away, Desiree. Not 'til you get here."

Desiree yanked a U-turn from the shoulder of the road and, through a stream of tears, headed for Westside Oyster Bay.

Hush little baby, don't say a word. Mama's gonna buy you a mockingbird.

Her body clamoured for air. She opened all four windows and stepped on the gas.

Poor Sully. She's confused. And I yelled at her. I yelled at poor Sull.

Desiree couldn't remember life before Sully. She'd always been the other mother, in the other house, on the other side of the street. Her earliest memory of her now creeping back – sitting on Sully's knee – her tiny hand, hesitant but curious, reaching up to touch her unusual face. Desiree drove on, hair lashing in the wind.

And if that mockingbird don't sing

Chest thudding, stomach quivering, Desiree coasted into the driveway of her childhood home, the place of scattered newspapers and terracotta pots, the house of pleasantly cluttered corners. She lifted herself from the driver's seat and steadied herself on the open car door. A police cruiser and a tinted-window van were parked in the driveway. An unfamiliar stillness hung over the house.

"Dear child, I'm so sorry," cried Sully, as she rushed across the lawn, arms outstretched. "Doctor said it might have been the aneurysm, or maybe just a… a…" Sully wore a facial scar which caused a rigid tugging of her mouth to one side. Often mistaken for a smile, Desiree found it most annoying, especially at times like this.

Desiree's tone was flat. "Who's van?"

"Why… it's the medical examiner's, dear. Reverend Fry and the doctor have both come and gone. Your mother's being prepared for transport. The examiner is waiting for you."

A police officer was busy with paperwork in his cruiser. "What's he doing?"

"Just come inside," Sully said.

The pink lace curtains in Alice's bedroom window rippled in the morning breeze, gently coaxing her daughter along. Desiree stepped into the entrance way. The medical examiner stood politely to one side. His collapsible gurney was touching the plant stand. "You're crushing her African Violet." Desiree said to him. "Can you please not do that? It won first prize, didn't it, Sully… now where's that ribbon? It was right there beside it." She dropped to her knees in search of her mother's award.

"Come along, dear," Sully said, helping her to her feet.

"But he must have taken it," she replied, starring daggers at the man.

"Come now," she said. "Hold my hand."

"No. I'll go by myself," she said, swatting away Sully's hand. A pocket of cool air lingered in the hallway. "Mama," she whispered. As she fingered the textured wallpaper along the narrow corridor, the fear and anxiety of what lay ahead grew with each step. She reached the bedroom door, hesitated, then slowly moved her gaze to the bed. Desiree froze. It was the feet. The stiffened feet trapped beneath the quilt. The slack of the jawbone. The tangle of gray hair. The odd and penetrating silence. Desiree gripped the doorframe for only a moment and, unable to step any closer, pressed her hands to her stomach, turned and fled. Thumping down the basement stairs to the workshop, Desiree burst through the greenhouse, outside to Alice's garden. The stone bench sat vigil under the apple tree. The windchimes had fallen silent. Desiree sat and stared across the open expanse of the sea and it was then, at that precise moment, that a warm tickle of wind ruffled and lifted her hair, and a soft voice whispered, "I see it now, Desiree. It's a field of sheep."

CHAPTER 10

Desiree made no secret of her distaste for the Reverend Fry, and her mother's memorial service would not serve as a platform for his insufferable self-promotion. There would be no fear of God sermons, no sappy readings, no solicitation of any kind. Fresh peonies adorned the altar and rays of colourful sunlight slanted through the stained glass as Alice's friends took their seats. Sully delivered the eulogy, the Sunday school choir sang an uplifting hymn, and everyone joined in fellowship at the parish hall for a few refreshments.

A tentative plan was made for a private burial at a later date. Desiree's explanation for the Reverend was brief and to the point. "Mom's only sibling, her twin sister, lives in Boston. She'll visit later when she recovers from surgery. I'll decide then about a burial."

Desiree stepped into the parish hall kitchen. The ladies of the Women's Auxiliary were washing and wiping, sweeping and sweating, and packing leftover sandwiches into containers. "Thanks ever so much, ladies," Desiree said with a rueful smile. "A lovely job, as usual. Mom would be so honored. You even made her legendary cherry balls."

"Our pleasure, dear," one of them said. "The Auxiliary will miss her greatly. Here you go, these are the leftovers you requested. Your mom was always so proud of you, and the wonderful work you do." She began to stack the food containers into Desiree's arms which were already overburdened with bags.

"Mercy, what's that you're carrying there... oh Heavens, yes, the guestbook and sympathy cards. So many of them! What a lovely turnout we had. Here, I'll carry the containers and walk you to your car. Okay, are you ready, dear? Let's go." The two women exited the parish hall and struck out across the parking lot.

"What was I saying... oh yes, it's truly admirable, what you do. Feeding the hungry. Now, where's your car? Oh, way over there! My, but these shoes are a curse. It's my bunions to blame really. Calling for a bit of rain today. Badly needed, I must say. My poor cucumbers! Mind you, no one could grow cukes quite like your mother. Oh, here we are! Nice vehicle. Pretty color. Oh, watch your step, dear! DOG POO! Eww! Look, it's everywhere. Don't step in it. Now what in God's name is that? See? Over there on the ground? An old roasting pan, is it?"

"Darned if I know," said Desiree. "Thanks for helping me lug all this." She opened the hatch of her SUV and stowed away the containers as the woman wandered off.

"Come see," she persisted. "What's all that yellow liquid floating in this pan?"

"I really need to get home. I'm sorry," Desiree said as she slid into the driver's seat.

"Oh, of course, dear," she said as she returned to the car. "You must be exhausted. Now you take care and—"

"I will," Desiree said. The driver's window inched up and stopped.

"And drop by to see me sometime. You know where I—"

"Uh-huh."

Desiree keyed the ignition as the window closed the gap. The woman's lips were still twisting and turning as Desiree pulled away. Enough chit-chat for one day. Enough date squares and cold coffee to brutally sour her stomach. Enough bear hugs and hand squeezes to last a lifetime. What she ached for now was some much-deserved peace and quiet. But first, a quick delivery of sandwiches and sweets to Bayshore Drive, Town Centre. Late afternoon on a scorching day in June, Desiree was sure to find her usual gathering of gentle souls sitting in the shade of the enormous red maple, across from the soon-to-be-opened food bank.

CHAPTER 11

Aside from the tick-tick-ticking of the grandfather clock, the silence was deafening as Desiree roamed the rooms of her childhood. Any earlier dreams or ideas of keeping the house as a summer retreat had rapidly evaporated. The very walls and floorboards now conveyed an odd strangeness, the cozy corners and worn sofas now cold and barren. She wandered into the kitchen and phoned Alan, her newest volunteer, her man at the helm. Recently retired from the Port Sherman Police Force, Alan was seeking personal fulfillment in his golden years and fully committed to the opening of the Oyster Bay food bank.

"Hey, Alan. It's Desiree. I'm here at my mom's house over Westside."

"Oh, hi, Desiree. How was the memorial service?"

"It was okay, Alan. Very nice. Exhausting. Huge turnout, short service, and a ton of food. Glad it's over."

"If you don't mind my asking, what's the plan? For the family home, I mean. It was all so sudden. You must be up to your ears… and hey, listen, I'm just fine here, okay? No need to come in. I'm just following up on some paperwork. Things are moving pretty slowly with the opening, but we're getting there."

"Actually, that's why I called. At some point I'll be putting the house on the market and will sell the furniture and other stuff in an estate sale. But before I do that, would you bring the van over for this fridge and freezer?"

"Sure can! What's the address?"

"Might be some useful shelving here too. You can decide when you get here. I packed up some tins and dry goods. Expiry dates look fine. 122 Austin Road." Within the hour, the items were loaded onboard the Hunger Stop van bound for Bayshore Drive.

***

Meticulously sorting through her mother's personal belongings, Desiree wished to keep only her jewellery, a few heirloom dishes, and the beautifully illustrated *North-Eastern Wildflowers* book that Desireee had treasured as a child. She wept quietly as she lingered over her mother's notations pencilled in the margins:
Trout Lily. Seen along the path at the shore. 15 July
Sweet Rocket. Blossoming early this year. 12 June
Desiree picked violets for Daddy. 5 May

Alice's entire wardrobe of size 8 clothing was tenderly folded and packed in crates for the Port Sherman Goodwill Shop. The overstuffed filing cabinet of receipts, brochures, warranties, and bank statements could wait until tomorrow. Feeling anxious and lonely, Desiree crossed the street to Sully's house. "You need to tell me now, and don't be modest," she said, slipping her shoes off at the door. "Is there anything you'd like to have from Mom's belongings?"

"Oh, her windchimes, please, Desi. Many an afternoon we spent on that bench under the apple tree, eating fresh cherries and plums, solving world problems... and those chimes heard every word and would sometimes even add their own two cents."

"Windchimes it is," said Desiree.

"Oh, and her journal. Years ago, I gave your mother a journal for her birthday."

"Right. I remember that," she replied.

"She wrote in it every day, and always said if she died before me, I can have it back, you know, as a keepsake. We used to laugh about that." Sully's voice cracked. "But you don't think that day will ever come, do you."

"You've been an amazing friend, Sull," she said, touching her shoulder. "I'll be right back." Desiree left and returned with her mother's keepsakes. "I don't have time right now, but I'd like to read the journal myself someday, so I might borrow it back, if that's all right."

"Well, of course," Sully said with watery eyes. "Of course."

"I brought the African Violet too. I'll just kill the poor thing."

***

The liquidators required two weeks lead time to organize, advertise, display, and price the house contents, and the estate sale was scheduled for the weekend of July 6-7. Desiree was apprehensive of the notion of strangers wandering about her childhood home, picking through her parents' belongings, sticking price tags on her memories.

Nothing more than a bunch of pots and pans, furniture and old tools, but am I doing the right thing?

"You know, it's funny," she had said to Sully. "What I'd give for a sibling right now. So many decisions to make on my own. I didn't see this day coming. I loved being an only child. I mean, who wouldn't? Only when I started school did I learn that people take turns. I remember asking my primary school teacher 'What's a turn?' Can you believe that, Sully? What's a turn!"

***

With the estate sale fast approaching, Desiree was knee-deep in her final and most dreaded task – sifting through her mother's filing cabinet. Two recycling bags sat stuffed at her feet, plus a pile for shredding and a pile for refiling.
One more drawer. Now, what's all this?
Struggling with its weight, she lifted the first bulging folder onto her lap. *Christ Chronicles.* A pristine anthology of church newsletters dating back six years filled the bottom drawer. Desiree was dumbfounded that her disorganized mother would so painstakingly squirrel away this archive, in perfect chronological order, while loose pages of tax returns and insurance papers fluttered willy-nilly about the house. Before landing the entire contents of the drawer into the recycle bag, she pulled out the most recent issue, thumbed to its table of contents, and the words blistered up from the page like a bad rash:

FOOD BANKS: WOULD GOD APPROVE? Submitted by The Reverend Terrence Fry – Page 3:

In my modest opinion, no. God would NOT approve of food banks. Why? I will put it simply. God helps those who help themselves, and food banks encourage poverty. I am not suggesting we abandon our widows, orphans and war veterans, but they constitute a mere fraction of those living off our generosity. Are the impoverished not able-bodied men and women? Must we feel guilty when passing the panhandler in the street? Must my parishioners feel obligated to drop food items into a church bin before dropping their generous offerings onto the plate? No, and I daresay the Lord expects his children to make better of their lives. What kind of message are food banks sending to our young people? That it's acceptable to squander our precious, God-given lives on drugs and alcohol because there will always be free food? Food bins have been removed from the Church of the Holy Trinity and it is my hope that all pastors within our diocese will follow my lead.

Reverend Terrence Fry
Servant of God

Desiree let the publication slip from her fingers to the floor. It was all suddenly crystal clear, and she was fuming.

CHAPTER 12

Dan and Karla Duggan walked up behind their son, sitting slouched forward on the grass, a spread of white pubescent skin gleaming above his low-slung belt. His hair was shaved up one side of his head, and a wavy black mop on his crown flopped to the opposite side with a dyed streak of bright blue running through. Dan nudged him with his foot.

Matthew lifted a headphone from his ear. "Wha'?"

"The waterfront. Wanna come?"

Squinting into the sun, he asked, "Now?"

"C'mon," said Karla. "Let's take a prowl around our new stomping grounds."

After some hesitation, Matthew muttered, "Yah, I guess," and sprung to his feet. The three Duggans padded down Pinehill Avenue to the dock, feeling every part the newcomers, casting sidelong glances into the yards of their new neighbours. The street turned slightly to the east at the bottom of the hill and, in the shade of a mature and twisted white pine, they reached the crosswalk and proceeded across Bayshore Drive. Matthew had visited plenty of times, but now that he actually lived here, he was taking particular notice of its shortcomings. No skate park, no arcade, no canteen, not a teenager in sight.

An impressive display of yachts and pleasure craft were tied alongside the floating docks, while lobster boats and other working vessels bobbed and bumped against the government wharf. A stiff, salty breeze blew in from the bay as flags flapped noisily atop their masts. Seagulls watched intently from their perch on Captain Harry's Whale Watching sign. Karla wandered off to a sea glass kiosk, Dan headed for the yachts and cruisers, and Matt found a trash can to lean against, maintaining a safe distance from each parent.

Dan adjusted his sunglasses, plunged his fists deeply in his pockets, and in his best attempt at looking cool and composed, strolled alongside each vessel, stealing sneak peeks into the lavish cabins of the privileged. The personal items left on deck for all to see – the empty wine glass, the sunscreen, the bikini hung to dry – flaunting the very lifestyle he'd envied his whole life. "Hey, Matt! Come see this thirty-foot beauty," Dan shouted. Matt chewed furiously at a thumbnail. Dan walked over to him. "C'mon, son. Show some enthusiasm, for crying out loud," he said.

"Well, you're acting dumb, Dad! All nosey like."

Dan sighed and peered up and down the waterfront. "All right, let's go then. See if we can find mom."

Leaving the docks behind, father and son headed north along the waterfront to the shops. Outside the Pirate's Den, a boy wearing an eye patch plunged a plastic sword into Matthew's belly. "ARRRGH Me Bucko!" he sneered, before lurching away. Horrified, Matt started off after the boy. "Get lost! Ya friggin' little maggot!" he hollered as the boy disappeared from sight. Then, turning a blood-red face to his father, "What's so hilarious, Dad?"

"Chill out, my son! It was just a kid." Dan laughed.

"What's up with all the kids and baby strollers, and stupid cameras anyway? It's like everybody's on vacation."

"Yup," beamed his father. "They probably are!"

"Are they off those yachts back there?"

"Mmm, maybe, or tourists driving through, maybe even locals, I don't know," and turning in a circle with hands in the air, Dan exclaimed, "But I do know we're going to LOVE living here!" Matthew scowled as they picked their way through the colourful kites and windsocks and caught up with Karla outside the Hava Java Cafe. Cheerful families sat beneath yellow shade umbrellas, sipping coffees and buttering muffins. Through the open door wafted the aroma of freshly baked cookies.

"I'm hungry," grumbled Matthew.

"Pity's sake, we'll be heading home soon," said Karla, and with that bit of encouraging news, Matt felt a certain spring in his step. But they soon reached the end of the boardwalk, and there stood an antiques shop, The Wharf Rat.

"Well, we gotta take a peek," Dan grinned. "C'mon party pooper," he said, as he held open the screen door. Their arrival was announced by the tinkle of a bell and from a back room stepped a burly man with a full round beard the mixed colors of birch bark.

"He don't look like no rat," Matthew snorted.

"Shh, will ya," Karla hissed.

"How are you folks today?" the man asked.

"Never better!" said Dan.

"On the hunt for anything special?"

"No thanks! We're new in town and just taking a look around. Wow, would you look at all this neat stuff, Matt?" Dan's eyes scanned every wall, shelf and tabletop, that held old wooden figureheads, a brass porthole, a ship sextant, coils of rope, lures and hooks, ducks and decoys, and a toppling pile of wooden lobster traps.

"Do lobster fishermen still use this kind of trap?" Dan asked.

"Yep, sure do! But some find the wire mesh boxes easier to

stack onboard the boats."

Testing its weight, Dan lifted a trap a few inches off the floor.

"I take the weights out of 'em. Easier for me to handle, heh heh," said the man.

"How much?"

"I'll let that one go for twenty dollars, 'cause two of the wooden slats are broken. Tourists don't care about damage though. They'll pay anything for them things. Strap them to the car roof and drive hundreds of miles home."

Dan's gaze then wandered to the antique decoys lined up on a shelf. "Did duck hunters really use those things?"

"Oh, yes, sirree, back in the day, they sure did." The man limped out from behind the counter and lifted one down from the shelf.

"What's the piece of wood on the bottom for?" asked Dan.

The man's jaw dropped a fraction. "Why, it's the keel, son! Keeps the decoy upright in the water. You know? Like a sailboat?"

"Oh right, of course, like a sailboat… I just didn't realize a hunting decoy—"

"Ya see, the bird hunters carved the ducks hollow so they'd float, you know? Then they'd screw a flat bottom on, then add the keel. Where did you say you're from?" Dan ignored the old man's dig. "Some of these gunning decoys sell for hundreds. Collectors want them bumped and bruised, shot holes and all. This one's been carved and painted to look like the King Eider. Darned if I know how it landed around these parts. Eiders breed in the Arctic."

"Now isn't that interesting," said Dan, as the man balanced the decoy on its wooden keel back on the shelf.

Matthew shuffled from foot to foot, praying for the chime of a clock, an alarm, a tsunami, anything to end the history lesson. Karla walked to the light of the window and held up a blue glass buoy encased in a web of rope. "These are pretty, but why glass? Didn't they break?"

"Well, I reckon some did. They're called floats, glass floats. For the gill nets. Japanese made 'em first. Done by glassblowers back then. These ones here are replicas, of course."

Karla's eyes were everywhere. "Oh, look at that Dan," she said. "A driftwood picture frame!"

Matthew edged closer to the door. Dan hoisted the lobster trap onto the counter. Karla tumbled three glass buoys beside it and elbowed Dan out of the way. "Here, let's just carry everything inside the trap," she said. "Hmm, that brass lantern isn't half bad either," she mumbled and wandered off again. "Grab that duck decoy too, honey!" Dan hollered after her. "Might as well break the bank!"

The antique dealer watched with delight as the Duggans plucked item after item from his shelves. Carefully wrapping each purchase in newspaper, he stuffed them inside the lobster trap.

"This didn't start out a shopping spree!" laughed Dan. "Say, Matt? Think we can lug this up the hill?"

"No! We can't carry that thing home!" Matthew wailed. "Someone will see us!"

Karla leaned back against the counter, arms crossed, face grim.

"Here. Let's just slide it off the counter for starters," said Dan.

"I can't carry that up the hill! I don't have my puffer!"

Dan's neck reddened as he shot a quick glance and a forced smile at the shop owner. "What do you suggest we do?" he said through clenched teeth.

"Go get the CAR!" cried Matthew.

The antique dealer scanned the credit card and handed Dan his receipt. "No tax," he smiled, "for newcomers."

CHAPTER 13

Dan had the tape measure stretched from the garden shed to the back fence when Matthew ventured outside mid-morning. Karla was at the patio table where three shiny new garden trowels flashed in the sun, and fragile green vegetable seedlings awaited their fate in plastic trays. Enthusiasm was in the air.

"How come there's no cereal?" Matthew asked.

Dan retracted the tape with a zip and jotted the measurement on the back of his hand. "Not now, son! The topsoil's coming!" he beamed, furiously rubbing his palms together as though he'd won the lottery. Matthew frowned and looked with desolation to his mother.

"I can hear the truck now!" Karla said excitedly. "Let's grab the shovels!" Matthew watched in horror as his mother clunked to the shed in her rubber boots.

"I'm not shovellin' any dirt!" he hollered.

Dan's eyes darted about the yard. "We'll have some dumped right here, okay? I'd like some good soil up against the fence for my sunflowers."

"We're not planting sunflowers."

"How come? I love sunflowers."

"Yah, but I don't, so… no sunflowers."

Dan knew, in that instant, that he'd be poking a few sunflower seeds into the ground whether she liked them or not. Hell, he'd already bought the seeds. He tore the cardboard packaging from his stiff new work gloves. The approaching dump truck groaned noisily into low gear on Pinehill Avenue.

Matthew sprinted into the house, climbed the stairs two at a time, careened into his bedroom and clamped on his headphones. By the time the truck backed into the yard, the roar of its engine and the clanking of its tailgate was nicely drowned out by the whimsical, steel drum melodies of the Mario Brothers.

Crusts of a peanut butter sandwich had hardened on the plate, and afternoon shadows had lengthened across his floor before Matthew shuffled to his dormer window. To his amazement, his parents had shovelled, spread, and raked the entire truckload of black, rich soil into orderly garden beds. The seedlings, now wilted from their trauma, stood feebly in rows, hilled up with soil at their ankles. Karla mopped her forehead and swatted flies. Dan tossed stones into the wheelbarrow.

"What's for supper?" Matthew shouted.

"Come for supper? Oh, how thoughtful!" cried Karla. "We'll be right in! We're starved!"

"NO! I said WHAT'S for supper?"

"Oh, where's your PUFFER? We don't know! Where did you use it last?"

"You guys are WACKO!"

"He made TACOS!" cried Dan. "Let's wash up!"

Matthew turned his face from the window. He'd never want his parents to see him laughing. He was just thankful they were leaving him alone. He'd choose the empty stomach any day over that backyard hellhole of sweat and humiliation.

Just look at them down there, slaving away. And this is why we moved here? For mud and mosquitoes? Mom looks happy now though... happy-er, I guess. Grandma was right. I should've helped more, carrying groceries and stuff. And shovelling snow. All that stuff hurts unborn babies. Maybe if I helped more, everything wouldn'a happened. And I'd have a little brother.

***

Exhausted from the day's labor, Dan and Karla watched in disbelief as Matthew bolted down his second cheeseburger in three gulps. "It's like watching the wildlife channel," said Dan.

Karla shook her finger at Matthew. "No cell phone at the table." Annoyed, Matthew tossed it to the counter. His eyes then shifted to the serving plate. "You eatin' that last burger, Dad?"

"You go ahead, Son," said Dan. "I wouldn't want to lose a hand."

Then, without warning, across the table Karla launched a hissing grenade. "Let's all go to church!" she said. Matthew's head jerked up from the plate like a horse from a hay bale. Rocking back on the chair's hind legs, he watched in stunned silence as Dan kept chewing, staring straight ahead.

"Well, Dan? You're always nagging me to get out and about. It's a great way to meet people."

"So is joining a gym or taking sailing lessons," Dan munched.

Matthew held his breath. Dan's jaw snap-snap-snapped. After what seemed like an eternity, he swallowed, then shrugged. "Okay, why not."

The boy's hands flew into the air as his chair came slamming down. "Not cool! Totally not cool! CHURCH!" he croaked. "Can't you guys do something a little less brain-dead... like, I dunno, play washer-toss? Or bingo? You can't make me go to church!"

Over her coffee mug, Karla smiled serenely at Dan. "Sunday?"

"It's a date."

CHAPTER 14

Dan and Karla set out to attend Family Service at the Church of the Holy Trinity 'over Westside' where the mucky-mucks live. Towering white pines cast black morning shadows across the road ahead, and the mist rising over the golf course revealed signs of human movement on the greens. Karla's fingers tickled the salt air through the passenger window.

"I really need this," she said.

"Need what?" said Dan.

"I've not been right for years," she said. "This priest – this guy we'll meet this morning, Reverend Fry – I hear he does bereavement counselling. Spiritual healing." Dan's agnostic comments had landed him in enough hot water over the years, so he remained silent.

"Graeme would be starting nursery school this year," she said.

Dan reached over and gently took her hand. He'd learned the hard way that at times like this, it's best to keep it zipped.

"Dan?"

"Yah?"

"Can you show even a shred of interest at church this morning? Help me make a good impression? I want to be accepted. I miss that connection – that feeling of belonging as I had as a kid at St. Peter's."

"Will there be wine?" he asked with a grin.

Karla backhanded him across the chest. "No, dummy! It's

not communion service this Sunday."

"I'll try to behave, honey," he laughed. "You can count on me. I'll act all churchy-like, even if it means falling at the feet of the preacher and crying Hallelujah!" Karla didn't respond, but Dan beheld a dubious smile play across her lips.

Like new kids on the block, the Duggans nervously slid themselves into the back pew. Morning sun warmed the stained glass, setting houseflies abuzz on the window ledges. A fair-haired cherub of an altar boy lit candles. Like meandering pinballs, members of the congregation wandered haphazardly down the aisle, dropping one by one into their respective pews. They fussed with scarves. They fussed with silk ties. They fiddled with prayer books and hymnals. The scent of perfume and old money filled the air. Choir members, like sheep in satin robes, filed into their stalls and began the service with a three-part harmony performance of Karla's favorite hymn, *In the Garden*. Now feeling slightly more at ease, the Duggans settled in and enjoyed the morning service. On leaving the church, some folks nodded a courteous greeting, others offered a polite smile, but most of the congregation ignored the newcomers in their midst. Reverend Fry was pouring on the charm in the double doorway. "Hello, Bob, how wonderful to see you. Cured of the shingles now are we, Mrs. Isnor? Just look at our David – shooting up like a weed!" he crooned.

Dan and Karla stood aside waiting to introduce themselves and, when the crowd dispersed, the Reverend raised both hands in the air and swished toward them. "And to what do I owe the pleasure of these fresh new faces this morning?" he gushed and took Karla's hands in his.

"Hello, Reverend Fry. We're Dan and Karla Duggan, new in town," Karla began. "I used to attend St. Peter's in Port Sherman. My parents live there and are members to this day."

"Yes, yes," he smiled. "So glad you could join us. Welcome to Westside." He looked to Dan. "And do you have work here in Oyster Bay, Dan?"

"Actually, no. I commute each day to Port Sherman, but Karla has a virtual job, so to speak, so she works from home."

"That's quite a commute," the Friar remarked. "Where exactly do you work, may I ask?"

"The Health Authority," mumbled Dan. An unmistakable flicker of interest crossed the Friar's face.

"Brilliant! Well, I do hope you will join us again next week. Busy, busy! Saturday, two weddings! Sunday, family service with three baptisms! Women's Auxiliary Bake Sale at noon! You DO bake, Karla?"

"Well, I... let's say baking is not one of my—"

"Just drop it off to one of the ladies after next Sunday's family service! Wear a hairnet and remember, no peanuts!" he sang as he turned his back and whisked away.

Enthused and truly uplifted by the morning sermon, and with no particular reason to return home, Karla suggested they stop at the new oyster bar along the waterfront at Town Centre. Dan was overjoyed. He'd noticed a new brilliance in her eyes – a glimmer here and there – a hint of pink creeping into her cheeks. A glimpse of the vibrant woman he once knew. A bit of gardening and ocean air was beginning to show. Delighting in this slow but steady improvement in her disposition, he stole a glance at his wife in the passenger seat. Unsociable, unpretentious, nary a religious bone in her body, but somehow Karla had always found comfort in the church. And now, she's applying lipstick in the sideview mirror, wearing a stylish red dress, and wants a lunch date!

Wow! Now if only she'd lose that stained, purple sweatshirt she wears to bed.

"Figure this place is open at noon on a Sunday?" asked Dan.

"I already checked the website," she chirped.

Dan held open the door as Karla ducked under his arm and stepped into the chic seafood restaurant. Rustic plank tables stood in sharp contrast to sleek counters and barstools. Oysters glistened on the half shell, chilling on beds of ice behind sparkling glass. Smooth jazz played in the background. Karla glanced around nervously. "This isn't one of those raw bars, I hope."

Dan ushered her to a table overlooking the bay. "Fear not. Cooking smells are drifting from the kitchen, but I insist you at least try an oyster." he said.

The waitress arrived with the menus. "How are you kids doing today?" she asked. Karla giggled and stretched the hem of her dress firmly about her knees.

"Wonderful!" Dan said. "My lovely wife here has yet to experience a raw oyster. Could we order a couple, just for starters? A taste test, so to speak?"

Gesturing to the oysters on ice, she said. "Those gems were in the sea just yesterday. Nothing fresher, nothing finer. I'll be right back." She winked at Karla. "You won't be disappointed. Shall I bring two glasses of white wine? I recommend the Chardonnay from the new winery."

"Whatever the lady desires," Dan said, smiling brightly.

Karla smiled demurely. "Sounds lovely. Bring the whole bottle." The Duggans chose shrimp linguine and seafood chowder for their main courses and closed the menus.

"You look really nice in red," said Dan.

"You think?" she said, glancing around the restaurant. "Oh, there it is. The washroom. I'll be right back."

Dan watched his wife walk away. She'd been wearing red the first time he clapped eyes upon her at the skating arena. She'd been but a speck in a kaleidoscope of girls skating by as he tightened his laces on the bench. Around the boards they came, squealing, holding hands, scarves trailing, tripping and stumbling on the ice. Dan stood on the ice and tested his steadiness as the girls came by again. The second time around, one girl had veered off on her own and lagged behind. Dan glided across the ice in her direction. Thickets of straight brown hair dropped in various lengths from beneath her stocking hat. Her bulky red parka grazed her knees, and her stiff white skates looked massive beneath the hem of her skinny jeans. To Dan's wonder, she stopped and smiled.

"Hi," she said, blowing furiously on icy fingertips.

"You can't possibly go to Sherman High," said Dan, "I think I would've noticed."

She dragged a sleeve across runny nostrils. "Nope," she said. "I'm from North End High. I'm here with those dopes." Her brown eyes danced as she giggled at her friends crashing into the boards.

"Wanna take a skate around?" asked Dan.

"Okay," she said, "but I suck at this. Don't hold my hand. Don't push me or pull me around, or anything, okay?"

Dan skillfully shifted into a backward skate. "I'm Dan, by the way."

"Karla."

Scraping and weaving their way through the moving crowd, Karla eventually took a spectacular spill. Dan careened into an elderly couple. They chased one another, hooted and high-fived, sipped hot chocolate from styrofoam cups and, by the time the three o'clock buzzer sounded, Karla's friends were in a collective snit, and Dan was in love.

***

Karla returned from the washroom, slid into her seat, straightened her placemat, looked across the bay, glanced toward the kitchen, and finally said, "What? Why are you looking at me like that?"

"Did you ever find your boots?"

"Huh? I'm not missing any boots. I haven't even unpacked our winter stuff."

"At the arena that day. Your friends hid them."

"Oh, that day. Those dummies. No, I walked home in my skates."

"And they never gave them back?"

"Nope, but you should have seen their faces on Monday morning when I showed up at school in two-hundred-dollar fur-trimmed Doc Martens."

"Hey," Dan laughed. "Come to think of it, I remember those!"

"Yah. Bless Dad. He felt sorry for me and took me boot shopping. But I doubt we ate much that week."

The waitress approached the table with an ice bucket, the wine and two glasses. The chef followed behind with a silver tray, two gleaming oysters sitting in pools of clear liquid on jagged half shells, a few lemon wedges, and a tiny bottle of Tobasco.

"Fabulous. My mouth is watering!" Dan laughed. He gazed up at the chef. "Say, these oysters aren't actually farmed here in the bay any more, are they."

"Oh no. That fishery closed down years ago," he said. "The bay is not clean enough, you see. The oyster requires pristine growing conditions, so they're now farmed in various coves and small inlets along the coast. Right now, I believe there are over a hundred active shellfish leases in the province. A thriving business. We are very fortunate. Enjoy your appetizers." The chef and waitress disappeared behind the swinging kitchen door.

Dan was the first to engage with his oyster. "You're supposed to sup it," he said pompously, "like this." He tipped the shell to his lips as a loud slurping sound filled the restaurant. "Go on then. Try yours."

Karla frowned at the oyster still jiggling on Dan's shell. "But you didn't eat the oyster."

"I will. After you," said Dan. Karla squeezed a lemon wedge over the sea creature, raised the shell to her mouth and supped.

"Not bad," she said. "Salty like."

"You didn't eat your oyster either," Dan said.

"Pour the wine first," she replied.

The Duggans sipped Chardonnay and watched sailboats leaning into the wind while their oysters waited on their shells. "Isn't this nice?" Karla said. "Lunch without the little grinch? I wonder what HE found to eat!" Bemused, she regarded the uneaten oysters. "You know what they say about those things, don't you?"

Dan brightened. "Why Mrs. Duggan, I do believe you are seducing me – and doing a fine job, I might add."

"No, seriously. Aphrodisiacs have been used for centuries to enhance the sexual experience."

Dan's face softened and he lowered his voice. "Yah? Well, with any luck the grinch won't be home and we could put that hypothesis to the test," he said.

Karla shifted in her seat. "Let's get these down our necks," she said. The two oysters finally met their fate and the Duggans were served their main courses.

Walking hand in hand back to their car, they heard a voice

call out from behind. "Hey, Dan, is it really you?"

"Adrian!" cried Dan as the two men noisily slapped one another in a man hug.

"You know my wife, right?" Dan asked.

"Sure do! We met at the first-year barbeque. Hi, Karla."

Dan grabbed his friend by the shoulders. "Congratulations, buddy! I planned to drop by the graduation ceremony but we were moving that day!"

"Moving? Oh, so you two live here now? In Oyster Bay?"

"Yah, just up the hill there," Dan gestured in the general direction.

"Oh man, did we miss you when you left nursing school! Are you coming back under the Special Circumstances clause? Surely, taking care of two sick parents must qualify you, right?" Dan frowned and shot a nervous glance in Karla's direction. Confused, Adrian continued cautiously. "Oh... so it doesn't qualify? You need to reapply?" Karla, having momentarily glanced at her cell phone now stepped forward with a renewed interest in the conversation.

"Nah! I got friends in high places, man!" He gave Adrian a playful but powerful punch to the shoulder. "So happy for you, Ade! Did you land a job?"

"Yah! Four of us got positions at the Health Authority. We started July 1."

"Did you get into orthopedics?"

"Yep! Sure did. So, listen, Dan, are you still interested in Emergency? Lots of positions opening up with the expansion of the Trauma Unit. Gonna be quite the facility."

"Yes, Emerg is still the plan," Dan laughed. "Don't ask me why, but all that turmoil and chaos appeals to me."

"Well, I don't mind sayin', you're making quite a name for

yourself in the O.R. The surgeons and anesthesiologists are always banging on about your magical powers. You walk on water, man! Get back into the program. You'll land a top nursing position, I guarantee you that!"

"Thanks, bud. I'll drop by orthopedics to see you." Dan watched pensively as his friend skittered down the boat ramp, strapped on his lifejacket, slipped into his kayak and paddled away.

"What was that he was saying about—"

"Aachh!" Dan scoffed. "Don't mind Ade. Doesn't know what he's talkin' about half the time!"

But the suspicion in Karla's eyes and the deepening knot in her brow told Dan that any glimmer of an afternoon tryst with his wife was all but flushed into the bay.

CHAPTER 15

Two Sundays passed before the Duggans returned to church, and the Friar was delighted to see them. He motioned for them to wait behind. "Aha, there you are. Wonderful to see you again."

"Oh," said Karla. "We missed a couple of weeks getting our house organized and garden planted. It's all starting to come togeth—"

"Cup of tea?" chirped the Friar. Dan was reluctant, but Karla appeared somewhat enchanted by the offer, so the Duggans followed him into his untidy office. A crooked bulletin board graced one wall, littered with yellow sticky notes, faded and outdated notices, newspaper clippings curled at their corners, and brochures stuck haphazardly here, there and everywhere, like a long-abandoned game of pin the tail on the donkey. On a table, a jumble of chipped mugs and dirty spoons lay beside an electric tea kettle. In a wicker basket, used teabags were tossed in with the new. Packets of sugar and whitener were strewn throughout the mess. The Friar brought the kettle to a half boil, dropped two bags into mugs, and drowned them in warm water. Dan and Karla stood awkwardly to one side. "Sweeteners, whiteners and stir sticks and spoons are all there. Take what you need," he grunted. "Nothing fancy, mind, but a good cuppa never disappoints." The Friar slumped down heavily in his armchair and waited. Like obedient pups, the Duggans clinked their spoons, and brought their mugs to his desk. "Do sit," he said. "Or take a load off, as you Canadians like to say."

Karla perched herself directly across the desk from the infamous Reverend Fry and, feeling quite privileged, politely sipped her lukewarm tea from her mug. Dan, however, having noticed the lipstick smear on his, placed it on the cluttered desk and remained standing. Reluctant to make eye contact, Dan fixated on the festoons of silver chains resting on the Friar's chest. The dandruff on his shoulders.

"So, you live up the hill from the waterfront, you say?" The Friar was making small talk. "The modest Cape Cod up Pinehill Avenue, is it? Corner of Jeffries?" A gaudy ring squeezed his baby finger, its silver serpent encircling and about to swallow the huge topaz gemstone. Leaning forward and clasping his spongy hands on the desk, the Friar breezed on. "So, you make that commute everyday, Dan, to the Port Sherman Health Authority, I think you mentioned?"

"Yup, that's right," he nodded. "Less than an hour to my desk." Dan did not like where this was going.

"And your occupation there?"

Clearing his throat, Dan was vague. "Bookings."

Karla piped up. "Dan works in O.R. scheduling. He can make anything happen around that place. Move mountains!"

The Friar slowly eased back in his worn leather chair and studied Dan's face. "Are you, by any chance, involved in scheduling the chronic pain clinic? Doc Durling's clinic?"

Dan crossed his arms in front of him. "Well," he said, "we actually have a very strict screening process—"

"Because, you see, my lower back has been quite bothersome of late, and my next nerve block isn't until October."

"Right," Dan nodded. "There can be quite a waiting list."

"Yes, of course. I do understand the simple concept of a waiting list, but surely you could pull a few strings for a man of the cloth?" Karla's brown eyes glistened as she looked eagerly to Dan for a response. The Friar remained toad-like in his armchair. Dan looked dumbfounded at the two of them.

"Well, that's not something I... I mean, I don't have that kind of authority." Karla looked up pleadingly at her husband, eyes wide, head tilted to one side. The Friar sat motionless – the heaving of his chest the only movement in the room. Dan looked once again in disbelief at Karla. She now wore the grimace that Dan knew well.

"Yup. Okay. I'll see what I can do," he muttered and headed for the door. Karla scrambled to her feet and followed.

"Fridays work best, and late in the afternoon would be brilliant!" sang the Friar.

Outside in the parking lot, Dan seethed at how expertly he had been reeled in. "Why did you encourage him like that, Karla? You know I hate doing this stuff." In his office, the Friar rocked back and forth in his squeaky armchair, smiling arrogantly, wholly oblivious to the sequence of events now set in motion.

***

Early Monday morning, Dan made the dreaded phone call. The bookings clerk in the Chronic Pain Clinic cheerfully answered her phone.

"Hey, Dan. How was your weekend?"

"Good. Hey, listen, there's a priority case I need to move up. Got any cancellations?"

"Ha! Ha! You're kidding, right? You know how tight it is around here!" she giggled.

"Do you have Friday's list in front of you?" He waited, fuming. "That last patient there, Lucy Halliburton, booked for

4.40 p.m., can you reschedule her?"

"No problem, Danno," she said, and assuming he was simply acting on the request of the pain specialist, Dr. Durling, she contacted Lucy Halliburton and postponed her appointment two weeks further along. The list was then revised and reposted to read: "Friday, July 15, 4.40 p.m. – Sacral nerve block – Terrence Fry."

CHAPTER 16

It was sweltering in Dan's office when his phone rang. "Dan? I need to see you. Drop everything. It's urgent." A writhing snake sprung to life in his belly as he rose from his chair. On shaky knees and, without making eye contact with a single soul, he made his way to the Administration Suite and tapped lightly on the door of the VP Medical Services.

"Come in, Mr. Duggan," said an unfamiliar voice. His fingers trembled on the doorknob as he stepped inside, and he was sickened to see the hospital's Chief Legal Counsel seated at a round table. Dan looked to the VP whose face was cold as stone. "Dan," the VP began, "there's been a complaint from the husband of a patient, and we need to get to the bottom of it. Right now." His mouth was a grim line. He motioned to a chair. "Sit."

"Okay," said Dan, faking a look of puzzlement, and he warily lowered himself into the office chair.

***

The interrogation dragged on to six p.m., and Dan's jaws were aching when the lawyer packed up her briefcase. "That's all for today," she said. "I'll be speaking with the family again in the morning, and I'll let you know our next course of action." Dan drove home in turmoil, slamming his fist on the steering wheel. "Damn, damn, DAMN!" he cried. "I knew it. I KNEW IT!"

Over dessert that evening, Karla said, "Wow, never seen you

this quiet. What's up?"

"Yah." He faked a yawn. "Just super busy at the office. Can't seem to shut down."

"So, I was wondering how much we'll need for your third-year textbooks. I've got some money put aside... been a good month. I've done over two hundred surveys." Karla noisily scraped the remaining film of ice cream from her bowl. "You're going to need some new clothes too, or do you wear mostly scrubs in third year?"

"Ah yah! Textbooks! I'll check out some used ones."

"Were you able to get Reverend Fry's appointment moved up?"

"Done."

"Aw, that's just great, Danny. I had my first counselling session with him this morning. My next session is Wednesday. He's quite charming when you get to—"

"Hey! I noticed you planted flowers in the lobster trap. Petunias, are they?" Dan peered intently through the kitchen window.

Karla looked at him suspiciously. " Yah," she said. "How very observant and, in case you missed it, I also served our own garden peas with supper."

"Oh. Right. Delicious, weren't they? Those seedlings shot up crazy fast, huh?"

"Sure did. I sent Matt to the garden to pick them but he came back with an empty bowl. I had to take him by the hand, swear to God, lead him to the peas and teach him to snap off the pods. And you know what he said?"

Dan managed a rueful smile. "What did he say?"

"You never told me they looked like that, Mom! Peas are supposed to be round!" Karla's eyes danced as she playfully swept the dishes from the table.

"Well, to be fair," laughed Dan, "the ones in the tin cans ARE round!"

"Yah, I'll get him good tomorrow. I'll tell him to go pick some corn niblets... oh Danny, can you even believe that kid of ours?"

***

Dan's pillow was sodden with sweat when he awoke the following morning. Minnows darted here and there in his stomach as he drove, and a message was flashing ominously when he arrived at his desk. "Dan, come down as soon as you get in." The VP was waiting, and he handed Dan an envelope. "Fortunately for the hospital, the family has withdrawn its complaint."

"Whew," said Dan, looking sheepishly at his superior.

"Unfortunately for you, they did so on condition of your termination, and we have agreed to that." Waves of heat washed up his neck as Dan slowly turned his reddening face to the voice speaking from behind.

"You'll need to come with me now, sir."

The VP returned to his desk, Dan surrendered to the security guard, and the rest of the journey through the corridors and up the elevator was like a disturbing dream – flitting images, moving in and out of focus. Upstairs in bookings office you could hear a pin drop as Dan was escorted to his desk like a convict to the gallows. Wide-eyed, nudging and craning, his co-workers gawked at the spectacle. Jinghua blinked from behind her bangs.

"Pack up your personal belongings, please. Do NOT touch the computer. Just gather your things." All eyes burned into his back as, meek and humiliated, Dan walked out the door with his sorry little grocery bag of office trinkets.

***

Dan had no recollection of leaving the parking lot nor driving home. He did, however, remember picking at his dinner and emptying two bottles of wine. The rest of the evening was a blur. A sickening blur followed by a sleepless night of torment. The following morning, Dan dragged himself from bed, prepared for work in his usual way, deciding to say nothing to Karla. Not yet. After driving aimlessly in circles for over an hour, he finally bought a coffee in the west end of the city and slumped down at a picnic table beside the drive-through. He tossed his car keys and phone on the gritty table and was prying the lid from his coffee, when the phone vibrated. *Jinghua Calling.*

"Aw, shit," he muttered. "Yah?" he answered.

"You okay?" she whispered.

"Stunned is the word, Jing."

"You know why you got fired, right?"

"Ah yah. I screwed up."

"Dan. Who ze heck is Terrence Fry?"

"Our stupid priest."

"Huh? What were you thinking?"

"Eternal salvation. I dunno!"

"You know what else happened, right?"

"Um, no, Jing, Actually I don't, but you'll enjoy telling me."

"That lady you postponed? Lucy Halliburton? It was the second time she got bumped. She could not wait two more weeks, Dan."

"What do you mean, she couldn't wait?"

Silence.

"Couldn't wait for what? Jing?"

"She commit suicide."

Dan's blood jumped in his veins and ran cold. Sounds around him became distant. A cramp wound its way through his gut. "She what? No, Jing. Please. Please, no." Jinghua remained silent.

Pacing across the parking lot, twisting his curls from their roots, he managed to mutter, "Karla. This is all her fault. No. No, it's not. It's the stupid priest's fault! He made me. He made me do it," he whined.

Silence.

"Jing? You still there?"

"Yah, Dan"

"My fault. My stupid fault. I did this." His voice cracked, "that poor lady… I have to hang up."

CHAPTER 17

Depressed and ashamed, Dan sat in the reading area of the Port Sherman Public Library. Having spent the past two hours agonizing through the fine print of the Provincial Unemployment Standards, he'd never felt so demoralized. His cell phone shuddered in his pocket. Jinghua again.

"You stalking me?"
"How did Karla take the news?"
"I haven't told her."
"Dan, naw you listen. You have to tell her. Let's have a beer. I'll buy. Where you now?"

Always keeping a safe distance from hospital and university, Dan suggested they meet at the pub next door to the library. Over several beers and a shared plate of chicken wings, Dan rehashed the entire nightmare. He pushed his dismissal letter across the table. "Read for yourself. Professional misconduct. I got off easy. Should have been involuntary manslaughter."

***

Dan found the public library as good a hideaway as any, as he continued to fake his daily routine – leaving the house at the usual time and staying away the required number of hours. He kept in daily contact with Jinghua, but she wasn't always a rock-solid pillar of support.

"Aw," she teased, "all fawgotten soon. You be jussa memory

round here."

"Jing. Did you happen to hear how she… you know…"

"Who? Who did what?"

"Jing, please. I need to know. I'm dying inside."

"The Halliburton lady? Don't torture yourself, Dan. No one knows how she took her life."

"Are they filling my position anytime soon?"

"Ahh… not sure, maybe reorganize. I take on most of your workload. We don't handle chronic pain any more. Oh, and did you hear what the scumbug priest told Doc Durling?" Jinghua lowered her voice. "Juss wait, I go downa hall." Dan rubbed furiously at his forehead while Jinghua skipped along on her teensy-toes, voice muffled in the corridor. "Okay, you still there, Dan? That priest! What a scumbug."

"BAG, Jing. ScumBAG."

"Okay," Jinghua whispered. "When the priest came in for his nerve block, he told Doc Durling you insisted on fast-tracking his appointment! All YOUR idea to postpone that lady."

"WHAT!" Dan's eyes darted about the library as he lowered his voice to a hiss. "How do you know all this?"

"Doc Durling told us herself! At chronic pain meeting… you still there, Dan?"

"Yah."

"Not good. Nobody knows who to believe."

Dan's jaw tightened and his voice rose an octave. "Well, you know who to believe, right? Jing?"

Silence.

Dan felt his face twitch – his upper lip curl against his teeth. "I hate him," he seethed. "I hate the bastard."

***

It was well after midnight. Dan sat alone at the kitchen table, a triple rum in hand, staring at the newspaper rolled in its plastic sleeve. With thoughts rambling, he was, quite suddenly, startled by the mindless power he once possessed. Mechanically shifting and postponing patients at random. Names without faces. Shuffling and rearranging, with no regard for their own personal struggles, the mountains they'd climbed, the obstacles they'd overcome, the pain they'd endured, the wages they'd lost. Individuals who turned their lives upside down just to land on that operating table. All down to Dan. Dan and his wonderful spreadsheet.

He unfolded the newspaper and thumbed to the obituaries.

Lucy Lynn Halliburton, 33, of Port Sherman, died suddenly at home after a lengthy illness. She is survived by her husband, Christopher Halliburton, and two sons, Byron 6, and Michael 4. Cremation has taken place. Memorial service will be held..."

Dan emptied the glass with a final swig and softly moved a finger across her photo. "Lucy," he blubbered. "I did this to you, Lucy." His forehead hit the table and sometime later, in his rum-infused dreams, her face looked strangely peaceful.

CHAPTER 18

The sweet scent of fresh rain on newly mown grass wafted on the breeze that gently lifted the curtains beside Karla's desk. A distant roll of thunder turned her thoughts to Matthew. He'd gotten up early, bolted down his toast and jumped on his bike to see the grand opening of some new sports outlet up Route 14. She frowned at her watch.

Sure as heck, he'll be caught in a downpour.

She'd get a few surveys done, then text him. With a grunt, she slid the red binder "Labour Market Survey" from the bookshelf and pulled from the desk drawer the list of Canadian citizens randomly selected to answer the thirty survey questions. Starting midway through the Os, she dialed a phone number, leaned back in her chair and gazed out the window. A jagged bolt of lightning flashed in the sky.

"Hello?"

"Hello, am I speaking to Mrs. Colleen O'Hearn?"

"Yes."

"Are you aware that you have been selected by Statistics Canada to participate in a labour market survey and that it is mandatory for you to participate?"

"Yes, I am," she said proudly. "I received the letter a few weeks back."

"Is now a convenient time for you to answer the survey questions? It will take approximately fifteen minutes."

"Yes, please go ahead."

"Are you the only person living at your address?"

"Yes."

"Are you currently employed?"

"No."

"In the past fourteen days have you applied for employment?"

"No, I have not."

"In the past fourteen days, have you been offered employment—" Karla hesitated, confused, as a sudden chill ran through the room. "I do apologize, Mrs. O'Hearn." She began again, "In the past fourteen…" Her voice trailed off.

"Yes? I'm still here. Hello?" Mrs. O'Hearn's voice became strangely distant as a breath of icy air settled between Karla's shoulder blades.

"Miss? Are there more questions?"

Sideways like a crab, Karla scuttled her office chair to the window and slammed it shut, but the frigid air lingered behind her like an open freezer door. Goosebumps lifted on her forearms. A nest of tiny spiders scurried up her back. The receiver fell from her hand. "Hello? I'm still here," Mrs. O'Hearn rattled on through the telephone wire. "Hello?" Terrified to turn around, Karla hunched forward to the computer, tugging her shirt collar up and around her ears. A dark shadow passed behind her in the reflection of the computer screen. Petrified, she hit the power button. The screen went black. "Hello? Is the interview over?" File folders fluttered open – their contents shifting and shuddering in the air currents. Karla frantically slapped them down. "STOP! STOP!" she cried. Dizzy and disoriented, wheeling backwards in her chair, she hurled herself into the corner, smashing a plant pot and scattering soil across the room. Lifting her bare feet from the floor, and squeezing her knees against her chest, Karla remained crouched in the corner until her respirations slowed, the papers lay still, and the heat and humidity of the summer rain returned warmth to her tingling flesh. When the porch screen door slammed, Karla's heart jolted in her chest.

"MOM! WHERE'S THE TIRE PUMP?" Matthew howled.
Deep breaths. Deep breaths.
"I GOT A FLAT ON THE BIKE! HAD TO DITCH IT DOWN THE HIGHWAY!"
"I'm in here."
Matthew squeaked in wet sneakers across the floor to the office. "I gotta go get my bike – hey, what's wrong? You sick?"
"I'm okay. Hang up the phone, will you?"
Matthew placed the receiver on its cradle. "Why is there dirt everywhere? And who shot you with the stun gun?"
"The pump's in the shed. Go get your bike before someone steals it."

When the door slammed behind her son, Karla managed, on trembling legs, to climb the stairs to the medicine cabinet. Two Diazepams eventually settled the shakes but did nothing to explain the occurrence.

Later that evening, Karla tried to explain the terrifying incident to Dan, but he did little to ease her frightful state of mind. "That was a cold front," he said. Attempting to demonstrate two layers of air with his hands, he continued. "See, a cold front moves in like this, pushing the warm air up, and when the warm air goes up," he leveled a hand above his eyes, "its temperature drops, forms ice balls, and it comes down like hail. Sometimes as big as ping-pong balls."

"You're not listening to me, Dan," she said. "It was INSIDE the house."

Dan furrowed his brow. "It hailed inside the house?"

CHAPTER 19

As executive director of HungerStop, Desiree often worked fifteen-hour days at its Headquarters and Distribution Centre in Port Sherman, pushing herself beyond the call of duty at every level. A powerhouse of energy in a high-profile position, she organized county fundraisers, sat on several committees, served as government liaison, managed over fifty sponsorships, and accepted several speaking engagements per year.

Desiree had inherited her mother's small build and green eyes, but her hair color was always subject of lively debate among her co-workers and she good-naturedly enjoyed the attention. "Oh, I don't know. What color would you say it is today?" she would tease. "Really? Was my hair red yesterday? I can't seem to remember." She found it all a most wonderful and welcome stress-reliever.

Extremely accomplished for her twenty-five years, Desiree was financially independent, unattached, and a tireless worker. Personally committed to the cause, she often topped up the warehouse food shelves from her own kitchen cupboards when donations ran low. Her utilitarian apartment in downtown Port Sherman afforded her the opportunity to bicycle to work, and she was renowned for jerking her bike to a squeaking halt on the sidewalks to chat with panhandlers, and to drop off perishables that would otherwise go to waste at day's end.

It had been a month since the estate sale and Desiree had many loose ends to tie up. Exhausted and having made several stops on her way home from work, she stepped into her apartment, dropped her bags, kicked off her shoes and sent them spinning. A single message flashed on her phone.

"Desiree. Hi, it's Sully. I need to see you. I found a note from your mother, and well, she didn't do anything bad, like against the law. But, oh dear, she did something without your knowing, and without your dad's knowing, but like I said, it's not bad. Just call me."

Desiree threw back her head and pleaded with the ceiling. "Please, no. What now?" she whined. She yanked a bottle of wine from her backpack, slid it into the fridge and returned the call. Extreme fatigue and frustration were obvious in her tone. "Sully, what do you mean you found a note? Where was it, and what does it say?"

"Desiree, okay listen, you're absolutely sure everything sold at the estate sale. Right? Everything?"

"Yes, everything sold! They auction the stuff in groups. You know, all the tools together, all the dishes together, all the gardening stuff, but, Sully, I told you all this."

"But you weren't actually there. You didn't see who bought what."

"Of course not. I left it to the professionals and vacated the premises. I was an hour away pacing circles here in my apartment. What the hell's going on?"

"I can't tell you over the phone. Can you come see me in the morning?"

"All the way to Westside Oyster Bay? I have a ten a.m. meeting here in Port Sherman."

"It's important."

"See you in the morning," she sighed. Desiree popped two sleeping pills and spent the next eight hours oblivious to her own curiosity.

***

Sully was wringing her hands when Desiree arrived. "Come in, dear. Coffee?"

"Well, how long is this going to take? I need to get back to the city." Desiree's gaze moved to the kitchen table. "Is it something you read in Mom's journal?" she asked.

"No, Desiree. Not a journal entry. A note tucked inside it. Sit down, dear." Sully opened the cover of the journal and smoothed her hand across her own inscription. *To my friend, Alice, keep recording your daily activities. It helps me remember things! Happy Birthday! Your partner-in-crime, Love Sully.* A smile spread across her face as she recalled giving Alice the gift.

Desiree fidgeted in her seat. "Well? The note?"

Sully was clearly distracted. She opened to the first page. "It was tucked right in here," she said, "slid right out onto my lap."

Desiree grimaced at her watch. "So, where is it now?"

"Hmm. Let me see... now where in tarnation did I put that?" she mumbled as she wandered off.

"Just tell me what the note said. What did Mom do that's so earth-shaking?"

"Oh, here it is. Right beside the phone. When I called you last night... I put it right here. I'm getting so forgetful. Now, give me a minute, dear. Let me find my glasses."

Desiree snatched the note from Sully's hand, and read her mother's familiar handwriting:

My dearest Sully: "I hope you have found this in time. In case I should die suddenly, there is something I need to confess. After Archie died, I did something he had absolutely forbidden. As you know, he's always been terribly opposed to..." Desiree read on in dismay, her eyes like whirlpools. "No, Mom! It's too late, too late!" she cried, her facial expressions shifting and changing shape like clouds across the sky – anger, shock, sadness, fear. After a few moments of silence, she folded the note and handed it back across the table. "Well, this is a fine mess," she said.

"Just tell me what to do," said Sully.

Desiree paced the room. "Oh, Mom, why couldn't you just honor Dad's wishes? Now we have a problem, a huge problem, but I'll fix it, silly mother, I'll fix it." Fumbling through her purse, she pulled the business card of the estate agent and dialed the number. She groaned at the automated phone message.

"Hello. You have reached Truemann Auctions and Estate Sales. For service in English press 1, Accounts press 2, Bookings press 3, to speak to a representative, please press 4." Minutes passed. "Hello, Truemann's, how can I help you?"

With enough sarcasm to sour milk, Desiree asked, "What number do I press for sick and tired of waiting?" Sully winced and shook her head. Desiree drew in her claws. "Um, hello. I do apologize." She cleared her throat. "This is an unusual question, I realize, but if I needed to repossess an item sold at an estate sale, what course of action could I take, if any?"

"Well, Ma'am, that could be a bit of a challenge. Did you not sign a release statement on the contents of the estate?"

"Yes, but I've since learned of the enormous sentimental value of one of the items."

"Did Truemann's handle the estate?"

"Well, yes! Why else would I call Truemann's?" She crunched her face at Sully and shook her head in disbelief.

"Where and when was the sale, and who is calling, please?"

"Estate of Alice MacLeod, 122 Austin Road, Westside Oyster Bay, July 6 and 7. I'm Desiree MacLeod, her daughter."

"You must understand that, unless you can locate the person who purchased the item, there would be little we at Truemann's could do to assist you. Can you describe the item for us? Perhaps one of our agents will recall the purchase."

Desiree provided the information and hung up. "I'm not going to make that ten o'clock meeting. Can I stay here a while, Sully?"

"Of course! You can't be alone at a time like this!"

Truemann's called back. "I spoke to the agent who oversaw that particular estate sale but, as expected, he does not recall the item, Ma'am. I'm sorry."

"So where does that leave me? How can I find who purchased it?"

"For a start, may I suggest you place an advertisement in the antiques and collectibles newsletters. There are a few publications in circulation."

"Um, no! That would take too long. Do you have a list of dealers in the area?"

"Our files are confidential. May I suggest the Yellow Pages or online listings?"

"What are the chances that someone here in the Oyster Bay area bought the piece?

"A fairly good chance, I would guess, Ms. MacLeod."

Desiree hung up the phone, buried her face in her hands, and began to heave and shudder. Muffled sobs escaped her fingers. Sully sat down with the box of tissues and placed her hand on Desiree's knee. "Cry it out, dear. We'll find it. Everything will be just fine now, don't you worry," she soothed. But when Desiree dropped her hands from her sopping wet face, she was laughing hysterically – her lips a gooey mix of spit and tears. The sofa beneath them shivered and shook as the two grieving women convulsed in laughter, hooting, snorting, and gasping for air. Finally, when Sully was able to speak, she threw her hands into the air. "WHO, Desiree?" she cried. "Who else but your mother would DO such a thing!"

CHAPTER 20

The scraggy boy seemed to pop straight out of the asphalt, airborne on his BMX bike.

"Hey," he said to Matthew, bouncing to a stop.

Matthew wiped his mouth on his sleeve. "How's it goin'?"

"Name's Leevon."

Matthew stared at the asphalt. "Like… in the song?"

"Yah," he shrugged. "Like in the song. With a double E for emphasis. LEEvon."

"I'm Matt," he said.

"Like on the floor?" Leevon grinned.

"Huh?"

"Never mind." Leevon eyed the oozing donair mangled in Matt's grip. "Where did ya buy that?"

Matt gestured to the new kiosk on the dock. Leevon pawed at his pockets for change. "You live here?"

"Moved here in June." He gestured across the street. "Up Pinehill Avenue. You?"

"Just down the highway at the campground. I stay with my mom in the motor home, but only in the summers." He dropped his gaze to Matt's skateboard on the ground. "Nice board, dude! I'll bring mine tomorrow! What say we terrorize some tourists?"

***

Over the course of the summer, the two boys became fast friends. Weekends typically found them at the campground, sprawled out on lawn chairs watching the big rigs and RVs rolling in, license plates from all over the continent. Balmy evenings of bonfires and karaoke, and a steady stream of pretty faces left Matthew and Leevon feeling lost each Sunday as the weekenders pulled up stakes and headed home through the campground gates. In the quiet aftermath of one such lively weekend, the boys sat baretorsoed in the window of the motor home, crunching noisily on their breakfast Shreddies. Outside, Leevon's mother stretched lazily on a lounger with her tea.

"Does your mom always wear those Elton John sunglasses?" asked Matthew.

"Pretty much, yah."

Matthew gazed across the trampled grass and burned-out bonfires to the campground washrooms. "Is she done cleaning the toilets and stuff already?"

"Oh, she does that late at night," said Leevon.

"Does she have other jobs?"

"Yah, she works undercover."

Matthew's spoon hovered over his bowl. "Your mom's a cop?"

"Nah," Leevon laughed. "She's the clown outside the flower shop."

"The one handing out roses?"

"Yup, that's her. She's also the rubber duck at the car wash, and the Mexican in the sombrero at Burrito Jax."

"What's her name again?"

"Gemini... or just Gem."

"She's cool."

***

Throughout the weeks, the boys loafed around the waterfront, always into some kind of mischief, snickering at seniors hobbling off the buses or pitching stones at seagulls. One evening, after rumbling up and down the boardwalk on their skateboards, a thick fog rolled in and they collapsed on a bench under the greenish glow of a street lamp.

"Ya know, my mom told me lots of stories about this creepy town," said Leevon.

"Oh yah? Like what?" Trying his best to sound offhand.

"Like this freakin' zombie, right? His clothes are all, like, tattered and soaked in blood. He comes around here at night after everything's closed. Rattling all the doors. Lookin' in the windows."

Matthew cast a frightened glance toward the waterfront shops. "Those doors and windows?"

"Yah. Those ones."

"Does he come every night?"

"Foggy nights mostly."

Leevon's shoulders hunched against the dampness of the bay behind them, his face an eerie green. "Then there's the drowned kid."

"Oh yah?"

"Yah," Leevon said, shooting a glance over his shoulder. "A little kid drowned here, like, forever ago." Lowering his voice to a whisper, he continued. "People in their boats at night have seen, like, this white glow on the water. Then, when they come up alongside, there's like this little dude floating under the surface, staring straight up, except his eyeballs are all chewed out by crabs and stuff. Chewed right out of their sockets."

"Oh man, that is SO awesome. I love this town," said Matthew, but when they parted ways at the crosswalk, he yanked up his hood, crushed his skateboard under one arm, and ran helter-skelter up the hill. For the next week he slept with his lamp turned on, and a T-shirt shoved under the door to conceal the glow.

CHAPTER 21

Fearful that Karla would become suspicious of his movements, Dan made certain the mileage on the car was in keeping with daily trips to the city. Waiting patiently at the gate for the Port Sherman Casino to open, he recalled the day he had scorned Karla for gambling at the corner store. "Oh relax, Dan. It's just a scratch ticket," she had laughed, scraping the coin back and forth, back and forth, and blowing away the residue. "There. You see? A free ticket!" Little did Dan know at the time he'd soon be dropping hundreds – daily – to feed a slot machine addiction. Chipping away at his parents' hard-earned savings, dollar by dollar, hour by hour. One more pull. Just one more.

Whirrr! Orange Lemon Cherry
Whirrr! Orange Cherry Cherry
Whirrr! Lemon Lemon Lemon
DING DING DING!
Dan was hooked, and badly.

Dan justified his spending by convincing himself that if he wasn't playing the tables, he wasn't, in the true sense of the word, gambling. Intrigued by the sombre, smoky, poker players, he would often linger at their tables to watch. Dan envied the lifestyle, the mystique, the tension, the private jokes. He watched the dealer's slim fingers skilfully flip the cards in front of each player. She was captivating and exotic. Her sleek black hair swung rhythmically as she leaned in to each player. Her smile was as white as the crisp shirt which clung tightly to her body under a black satin vest, cinched at her tiny waist. This morning, he watched from the shadows, back from the glare of the poker table lamp.

    The players fiddled with their poker chips. Clickety-click. Someone muttered. The others smirked. Clickety-click. Then Dan spotted it. Like an eyeball glinting eerily under the light – a gaudy topaz ring. Confused, he stared, then lifted his eyes to the face. The lips were all wrong. They curled back against the teeth, a wet cigar wedged between. And the hair was all wrong – thick and lustrous where there should have been a comb-over. Curly chest hair where there should have been a cleric collar. It coughed. It swirled whisky in a glass. It grinned like a snake. Dan's stomach took a leap. Behold the great imposter, the Reverend Terrence Fry! Dan was dizzy with excitement.

    Sweet Jesus. He's wearing a rug!

    Adrenaline pumped in his neck as Dan turned his back to the light and stole across the lush carpet into the darkness. Slipping his phone from his pocket, he thumbed open the camera. A security guard moved swiftly in his direction. Dan strode quickly back alongside the poker table, clicked three times, and fled to the exit.

CHAPTER 22

Karla was scraping the barbecue grills, when a tipsy Dan flip-flopped across the warm patio stones clutching two sweaty bottles of beer.

"Thanks, Mama. That was a mighty fine supper," he hiccupped.

"Yah? Was it really? What did we have?"

"Um, gimme me a minute," he grinned. "Pork chops?"

She eyed the beer bottles, frowned, and kept scraping. "I've been wanting to ask you something."

Aw shit. Not now.

"The bank accounts. Just wondering. Did you move some stuff around?" she asked.

"Move stuff? N-no. Don't think so." Dan's insides began to churn.

"I was doing some online banking today, but couldn't find the tuition account. You do have it all saved up, right? It's due on Friday."

Shit. The tuition.

"Um. We might need to talk about that."

She eyed him suspiciously. "Oh, this better be good."

"Can we sit? Have a beer?"

"Pity's sake, Dan. What have you done?"

"Okay, here goes." Dan blew out a shaky breath. "Karla, I lost my friggin' job. Okay? I haven't worked in weeks. Couldn't bring myself to tell you. I have no income. I have no savings."

His words fell like marbles from his mouth to the flagstones, rolling in all directions. Irretrievable.

Back and forth the brush scraped, side to side the ponytail swung, the rogue wisp of hair dancing and dangling about her forehead, never knowing exactly where to land. Dan waited.

"Karla?" he ventured.

The barbeque lid came down with a slam, as she ripped a beer from his hand. "What the HELL happened?"

"I really screwed up, honey."

She tossed her beer cap into the bushes and eyed his muscular brown forearms. "Jesus, Dan, where have you been spending all your days? And, and... what have we been living on, huh? Surely not my pittance!"

"Um," Dan cleared his voice. "The inheritance money... and the tuition money, BUT!" he continued, "I've already applied for unemployment insurance. Problem is, when you're dismissed from your job, the benefits don't begin until—"

"The INHERITANCE!" She glared at him in utter disgust, then stuck it to him hard. "Your parents must be so proud of their angel boy right now... rolling in their graves," she sneered. "You don't deserve a cent of their money! Pissing it away all summer. Exactly how much of it did you squander away?"

"A lot."

"How could you DO this!" Tears sprung from her eyes. "HOW?"

Dan shifted from foot to foot, waiting for a chance to speak. "You don't even wanna know what happened? How I got fired?" he said.

Matthew kicked open the screen door. "What the hell, you two? I could hear ya from way upstairs. Keep it down, or take it outside."

Dan threw his hands in the air. "We ARE outside! Go up and shut your window, find your damned headphones, shove beans in your ears, put a bag over your head. I don't care. Leave us alone." He turned to Karla. "So, answer me! You don't wanna know what happened?"

Karla's eyes burned into his. "Who cares? You screwed up! Then you hid it from me! Oh, all your little office fans are sobbing mascara tears now... especially your little China girl, whats-her-name, HING JING!" Karla yanked open the screen door and stomped inside. Dan stood dumbstruck for just a moment, then his blood came to a quick boil. He saw the Friar's greasy hair stretched like guitar strings across his bald head, the VP's cold stare, the obituary photo of Lucy Halliburton. Enraged, he burst through the door after her.

"YAH?" he shouted. "Well, if it weren't for you and your divine dimwit, it never would have happened, but hey, if you don't give a sweet shit!" He stood glowering, chest heaving.

"Who the hell are you talking about! Reverend Fry?"

"Ding Ding! We have a winner! Show the lady what she's won! YES, I MEAN REVEREND FRIGGIN' FRY!"

Karla hesitated, her lower lip beginning to tremble. "He got you fired?"

"Oh, nothing gets past you does it!"

Karla stepped toward him. "How? How did this happen, Danny? And why didn't you say anything?"

"I don't know. I don't care."

Karla took his hand. "Well, you'd be quitting the job in the fall anyway, right, honey? With nursing school starting back up? Right?"

"Yah, right."

Karla dropped his hand like a hot potato. "But you blew the tuition, Danny!"

"Hah!" he sneered. "I haven't fessed up to everything yet!

There's another bomb gonna detonate right here and now!"

Karla's face drained of all expression. "You're having an affair."

"Oh, don't put ideas in my head! No. It's nursing school." He crossed the kitchen, leaned heavily against the counter and defiantly folded his arms across his chest. "Guess what, Karla! I don't need textbooks! I don't need new clothes! Hell, I don't even need tuition! Know why? Wanna know why?"

"You're never going back," she said quietly as tears of shattered dreams rolled down her cheeks.

"You may now collect your prize," said Dan.

Karla mashed the heels of her palms against her eyes, wiped her nose on her shirtsleeve and pulled out two chairs. "Just tell me everything," she sniffed. "And start from the bloody beginning."

***

The kitchen table was littered with empty beer bottles when Dan and Karla finally took their pounding headaches and financial woes to bed. The discussion had been a brutal one – Karla reluctantly accepting partial responsibility for the whole Friar disaster, and Dan unwillingly admitting to a serious gambling addiction. With these two matters somewhat settled, the Duggans moved on to more fiscal matters, hammering out a temporary financial plan. Karla would contact her HR representative at Stats Canada and apply for full-time hours on the survey. Dan would find menial employment somewhere in Oyster Bay – preferably a cash job – so that unemployment benefits, when they did arrive, wouldn't be affected. Against the law, yes, but so is removing a mattress tag. There would be no fuel consumption, no trips to the city except for addiction counselling. Matthew would most certainly lose his allowance, and would need to land himself a paper route, sweep floors, or mow a few lawns to earn his keep. Their one saving grace – a mortgage-free existence – provided the cushion they'd need to muddle through. Curled tightly on his side, Dan stared at the dark outline of Karla's small figure in the bed beside him.

What a hellish, horrible night that was, but it's out. The whole nine yards. The whole day's catch. Helluva lot of heartache and pain. But no more lying. No more pretending. Oh my dying God, no more slot machines.

.

CHAPTER 23

Matthew thrashed between soggy sheets as the waterfront zombie rattled his bedroom doorknob. Awakening in a panic, he heard the car start up in the driveway. He crossed his bedroom floor and heaved open the window. Dan hollered across the yard from the car window. "Need anything else besides bread?" Karla wandered aimlessly about the property in her bathrobe, plucking a weed here, a deadhead there. She looked like death warmed over.

"I see you're both still alive!" Matthew hollered. "Who was the last one standing?"

Dan raised bloodshot eyes to the bedroom window.

"Jeez, Dad, what time is it? Aren't you late for work?"

"Hit the hardware store for a chimney brush," said Karla. "I think the chimney's full of soot. Then we'll light a fire later... try out the fireplace."

"Huh? It's the first of August."

"I know, but in case you haven't noticed, nights get damp and chilly down here along the coast. Now get going."

Matthew shook his head in disgust.

Why is she always such a bitch?

Yawning, he shuffled to the bathroom, but hesitated at the top of the staircase. Someone was whispering downstairs. "Mom?" He crept lightly down the steps and across the living room floor. "Mom? Are you inside?" He nervously glanced around the room as a gust of cold air fluttered at his pyjama bottoms. Matthew stood paralyzed as a cloud of gray dust drifted about his ankles before settling to the floor. His heart jumped as the door slammed and Karla stepped inside. "Who tracked that in?" she demanded. "I just swept that!" Karla looked suspiciously about the room. "What did you step in? Pass me the damned broom."

"Nothing," he said, "I didn't step in nothing." He dropped a PopTart into the toaster and texted Leevon.

9.10 *u up?*
9.11 *yeah comin down?*
9.11 *she there?*
9.15 *hottie from maine? yeah camper still here*
9.16 *how much?*
9.17 *30 for 7*
9.20 *later*

It was almost dinnertime when Matthew left the campground and headed back home. His warm buzz swept him playfully up the hill. Like a gentle pat on the butt. Up, up, up you go, up the hill you go, Maine-girl-with-the-birthmark's brother sells some bad-ass weed.

Leev's mom was smokin' it too. Man, I wish she was my mom.

He wished now he'd taken Gem up on the chili dog but he'd been jumpy and giddy, and real stoners don't act like that. It was time to leave there. Stopping to catch his breath, he sucked back two bursts from his puffer, dug into his pocket and fingered the plastic baggie and its crunchy contents.

I sooo ROCKED it with her today! AMAZE-ing birthmark. And I am totally gonna roll another joint. SOON as I get home! While Mom's getting supper... oh yeah! I am so BITCHIN' hungry.

Matthew rounded the corner to his driveway and stopped

short at the sight of his mother positioning a ladder against the house.

What the f—

"There you are!" she snapped. "Here. Get up this ladder."

"What for?"

"I'll pass up the chimney brush. Go on."

"How come Dad's home today?

"Get used to it. Now get up on that roof."

Matthew gazed up the ladder, rung by rung, chili dog by chili dog, stacked one above the other, all the way to the roof.

"Your father's in the fireplace holding the bucket. Just shove this brush up and down the chimney a few times, okay? Careful on the slope."

Matthew swallowed a high-pitched giggle. "Hell, YAH! I'll get up on the roof! Frikkin' right I will!" He started to climb.

"Hold it," his mother said. "You all right?"

"Pfft! Like, do I look all right?" Matthew clambered onto the roof, reached down, grasped the long-handled brush from his mother and scuttled up the slope.

"CAREFUL!" cried Karla as Matthew stood up, balancing himself on the peak.

"Ha! Watch this, Mom! I can fly!" Matthew tucked the brush under an arm and flapped one elbow. "Watch this!"

"Maybe you should come down," she said, clutching her sweater tightly around her.

"YO, DUDE!" he shouted down the chimney. "Little Danny Duggan, is that you down there? Santa Claus up here! Have you been a good boy? HA-HAAA!"

"About time you got home!" Dan hollered, craning his neck up the chimney flue. "Now cut the crap and push down the brush!"

I bet I could totally see Maine from up here. Vacationland. Coolest license plate ever.

He lapsed into a daze. What a stunner birthmark. A perfect purple teardrop, falling from an ocean-coloured eye... and she's blinking away the salty waves as they crash over her suntanned shoulders. And she's laughing. In vacationland.

"MATT!" came the voice from below. "Push it down!"

"Oops! Sorry down there, Danny Boy! Watch out! Here comes your lump of coal!" Matthew playfully pumped the steel brush up and down, up and down until the ear-piercing screech of metal-on-metal sent another shout up the chimney pipe. "MATTHEW! That's enough! Now, get down off the damned roof!" Matthew slid on his backside to the ladder. Karla waited on the ground. "What's up with you today?" she asked.

"I'll tell ya what's up! Me belly thinks me throat's been cut!" he beamed.

Karla eyed him suspiciously.

"You don't remember that movie line?" he laughed. "I'm HUNGRY, woman!"

***

Back inside, Dan and Karla gaped into the bucket. "Hmm... empty," Dan said with satisfaction. "Seems the previous owner was nice enough to clean the chimney for us."

Karla frowned. "Well, I'll be damned where all the ash around the hearth comes from." That evening, Dan crumpled newspapers and arranged sticks in the fireplace. After striking several matches and adjusting the chimney flue, a weak flame eventually jumped to life. Like children around a campfire, the three Duggans stood and gazed as the fire brightened and crackled, sending a galaxy of sparks up the chimney.

"Hey, this is kinda nice," said Matthew, somewhat surprised, and dropped himself into the deep armchair. "Way nicer than last night's war zone." With a clunk, Dan's heels landed on the coffee table and, leaning back into the sofa, he laced his fingers atop his cushiony curls. Karla peeled off her cardigan and headed for the kitchen. "Vino?" she asked.

Matt chimed in. "Can I have some? I was the one who brushed the chimney, and I was the one who went to the basement for wood!"

Of course not.

Having smoked another joint in the tool shed, Matt watched his parents with placid curiosity from across the room.

Married people in mind-numbing conversations, smiling through wine-stained teeth, turning the glossy pages of the seed catalogue. How pitiful is that.

All sounds in the room began to fade as Matthew drifted off, fingertips tingling on the TV remote. Brain cells deadening. Warmth and blackness flooding in. But then, from somewhere... a voice.

"Matthew, can you he-e-e-ar me?" it whispered. *"Wake up."*

Matthew's eyes darted beneath their lids as the voice crept closer. An icy breath drifted about his neck.

"Can't you see me? Look. I'm right h-e-e-r-e."

Matthew shrieked and hurled the remote across the room. His parents bolted upright. "WHAT?" Karla shouted, eyes wide with fright. The terrified boy pressed back against the cushions. Stabbing the air with his finger, eyes darting wildly about the room. "Th-th-at! That!" he stammered. "Did you hear that?" He swiveled his neck in every direction but whatever it was – whatever had set the blackbirds flapping in his chest – had sucked back into the void.

Karla attempted to remain calm. "You go on up to bed now, Matt. That was just a bad dream," she said. Matt needed no persuasion to leave the room and he bounded up the stairs three at a time. Trembling, lips numb, he slid between the sheets, and pulled his body into a fetal position.

Bad-ass. Bad-ass weed.

CHAPTER 24

As August entered its second week, Karla grew increasingly anxious about the happenings around the house. The episode in her office had left her nothing short of dumbfounded, and now Matthew had gone silent after his experience beside the fireplace. She and Dan were going to hash this out. Tonight.

Parting the curtains, Karla stood back from the window and watched her troubled boy, hunched on the back lawn, fiddling with a twig, his head bent, his sweet face gaunt, with the curve of his bony spine visible beneath his shirt. Her heart ached for the young Matthew, the raven-haired, bright-eyed, laughing boy who once filled their home with joy and laughter. When life was full of promise. Little Matty at the calendar with his green crayon checking off the days to Graeme's birth. Dan scoring top of his class in Anatomy, Physiology and Ethics. Life before moving in with the in-laws. Life before secrets. Sore, aching, tender secrets.

"A skim of ice on everything this morning," Dan had said. *"Don't step outside for the love of God. Don't check the mail or feed the birds or anything, okay, honey? Stay indoors. I'll be back in an hour. A few prescriptions to pick up, and we're fresh out of Depends. Again!" Such a caregiver was our Dan. But just one cigarette. On the front verandah before the old folks wake up. Just one. What harm can it do the baby now? Almost full-term. The creaking of the front door as she closed it behind her, the blast of frigid air, the click of the Bic lighter, the dizzying hit of nicotine, and the sudden terrifying crash. Housecoat flung wide,*

fingernails scratching and clawing at the thin sheet of ice, all the way down the wheelchair ramp.

Karla, highly accomplished in beating down spontaneous episodes of melancholy, wiped her tears and stepped outside. "Hey, honey," she said. "What time is Gem coming?"

"Um… soon I guess."

"Oh, here she is now."

Gem pulled her van into the driveway, as always, with two wheels off the asphalt squashing ruts into the lawn. "Hey, Karla!" she hollered through the driver's window. "I'll bring him home too! I'll be driving all the kids home."

"Thanks, Gem!"

Karla walked Matt to the car. "Have fun. Wish Leevon a happy birthday for me." Matthew slid into the backseat. "Don't forget his gift, doofus!" She passed the bag through the sliding side door and waved goodbye. The fog had taken its time clearing out that day, but the sun now unveiled the full splendour of Karla's purple asters and Dan's stunning sunflowers. A late-summer laziness hung in the air under crisp blue skies, as crickets took up their high-pitched drones in the trees. Karla had a lot to discuss with Dan, so she was pleased Matthew was spending the evening at the campground.

"What's going on down there tonight?" Dan asked after dinner. "More ghost stories around the campfire?"

"I sincerely hope not. Matt's traumatized enough," Karla said. "It's Leevon's birthday. Pizza party or something. Gem's bringing him home." Karla tucked a leg underneath her on the sofa. "Now listen, Dan. We're gonna talk about this, okay?"

"Oh, don't worry. I've been asking around but, with the tourist season winding down, jobs are scarcer than… what do they say? Hen's teeth."

"No, no. I wanted to talk about—"

"Well, I mean a guy down the street knows someone who might need help shrink-wrapping boats for the winter. And the B&B could use a handyman, but jeez, they want someone who can landscape, drywall, plumb, wire—"

"DAN!" We're going to talk about what's going on around this house."

"Oh, that," Dan tried to keep it light. "You been sneaking off to those spooky campfires again?"

"No time for jokes, Dan. The night we lit the fireplace and Matt dozed off... he heard something. You know that, don't you? And it... it wasn't a dream, Dan. Matt says it was like, like a voice, a man's voice, right here in the living room... DAN!"

"Whut?"

"Are you even listening?"

"Yah, yah, sorry." His eyes darted to the TV and back.

Karla grabbed the remote control and hit the power button. "As I was attempting to say, it's not the first time Matt's heard sighing and moaning around the house. He's scared, Dan. Your boy is scared."

"Well, how come he's never talked to me about it?"

"Because of this! YOU!"

Dan threw his hands in the air. "I don't believe in all that foolishness!"

"Listen to me. Matt's losing weight and... oh yah, and have you noticed his fingernails?"

"What about his fingernails?"

"Chewed to the bone, that's what."

"Karla. Listen. I don't feel a single bad vibe around this place. Nothing. So, nothing to discuss."

"Really? You think you can dismiss it that easily? Think again. Unexplained gusts of cold air. Eerie sounds. In my office that day... oh my God, Dan. Please listen to me. I have never been so frightened. I'm scared to be alone in the house now. Would you look at me, PITY'S SAKE!"

"All right, all right. I'm listening. I'm looking. Gawd, Karla!"

"I'm behind on my surveys, Dan. I'm afraid to work in my office."

"Seriously?"

"Yes, Dan!"

"Maybe you phoned a ghost that day," he grinned. "Maybe Mrs. O'Hearn drifted through the phone line and lives here now! With us! WOOO, what's that thump I just heard!"

Karla stared at her husband in disbelief. "Oh, you're a real comedian, you are."

"Well c'mon, honey. Get real."

"You know what?" she said, tossing the remote control onto his lap and marching off in a huff. "Just forget it. Just bloody well forget it!"

***

That night, Karla awoke and reached over to a chilly void on Dan's side of the bed. "Dan?" No response. She gathered her robe around her and crept into Matthew's room. As promised, Gem had returned him at midnight, and he was snoozing like a baby. Nervously, she called downstairs. "Dan? You down there?" No answer. On shaky legs, she descended the creaky staircase. "Danny?" A nightlight cast an eerie glow across the living room wall. Dan stood in his boxer shorts near the fireplace, staring through the window. Karla froze on the stairs. "What's going on?"

"I heard something," he whispered.

"Why didn't you answer me? Why are you whisper—"

"Can you see my reflection in the window?"

"What? No, Danny. I c-can't see your reflection from here."

"Come 'ere a sec."

"I d-don't want to," she whimpered, heart thumping in her ears.

"Karla."

"What... what is it, Danny?"

"Is there someone standing behind me?"

"No. Stop it. I'm scared."

"Come see," he said quietly.

She ventured nearer.

"Look." He reached a sweaty paw slowly behind him, grasped her hand and pulled her to his side. Resisting the urge to run and scream, Karla raised her eyes to the window as every hair on her body bristled. Silently standing behind them on the fireplace hearth was the shadowy figure of a slightly built, older man. He made not a sound, but his eyes met theirs in the reflection. Karla dug her fingernails into Dan's slippery hand and together they watched in horror as, like melting wax, the apparition slowly disappeared into the floor.

***

Agitated and sleep-deprived, Dan yanked on the covers. The clock read 5.31 a.m. A heavy object sat on the bed. Dresser drawers scraped open and slammed shut. Items of clothing flipped and danced in the morning gloom.

"What the hell are you doing?" he croaked.

"Getting out of here, that's what." Karla leaned over the bed and zippered the suitcase.

"It's not even daylight, where are you going? Where's Matt? Just wait... WAIT!" He struggled to sit up.

"Matt's already in the car."

Dan sprang to his feet. "Huh? Don't act so stupid. The poor kid, he's—"

"Get out of my damned way."

"KARLA!"

The suitcase thumped down the stairs and out to the back porch. The screen door let out a terrified squeal as she kicked it open and thundered the wheels across the patio stones. Matthew sat wide-eyed behind the foggy windshield, as Dan tried to pry open the locked door. "Matthew, it's gonna be okay, buddy," he mouthed through the glass. Dan pressed his forehead to the back windows and cupped his eyes with his hands. The backseat was heaped high with computer gear, tangles of cords, adapters, and binders sliding haphazardly to the floor.

With the strength of a stevedore, Karla launched the suitcase into the back and slammed down the hatch. Dan reached out and grabbed her wrist but her eyes, wild with rage, suddenly darted to the clothesline. Jerking from his grip, she flew barefoot across the patio and, with one rebellious tug, snatched her purple stained sweatshirt from the line sending clothespins spinning into the yellow morning mist. Dan watched dumbstruck as she yanked open the driver's door.

"You stay here in your little town," she sputtered and spit through angry tears. "Spend the rest of your inheritance, buy your boat, and drink your booze in your cute little, stupid little, haunted little house! We'll be at Mom's and Dad's."

CHAPTER 25

Thumbing through the yellow pages of the directory, Desiree located the list of antique and collectibles dealers in the locality of Oyster Bay. She estimated the catchment area to be about a twenty-kilometer radius around the town. She tore the yellow pages from the phone book and hit the road with her phone and GPS. Her plan was to begin the search around the periphery and work her way into Town Centre.

First stop. Hilltop Treasures. Eighteen kilometers to the north. The paved driveway swept through manicured lawns up to a stately home with a gabled roof. A carport connected the homestead to a small shop with red shutters, flower boxes and a welcome sign. Desiree opened the stained-glass door as a musical voice floated out from behind the counter.

"Hello, welcome to Hilltop. Come in, do come in." The woman slid the glass door on the cabinet, locked it, and pocketed the key. Turning to Desiree, and plucking the glasses from her face, she asked, "May I help you?" Showcases sparkled with vintage jewellery, pocket watches, music boxes, silver combs and hairpins.

"No thanks. Lovely shop. Just not what I was looking for." Desiree backed herself out the door. Hilltop Treasures. Check.

Captain's Cabin was another disappointment. Model sailboats, nautical flags, compasses, life rings. "Thanks anyway!" Desiree sang as she headed for the door. Captain's Cabin. Check.

She then headed inland to The Barnyard. Milk jugs,

weathervanes, wagon wheels, barrels, and pitchforks. The Barnyard. Check

In the parking lot, Desiree hunched over the steering wheel.

Oh, Mom, I WILL find it. I promise. But one more stop today, then I'm going home.

The last stop, BuyGones, was fifteen minutes west of town. Desiree crunched into the gravel parking lot and peered at the OPEN sign.

Oh boy. This will be a royal waste of time.

Yanking on the screen door, she stepped straight into a cloud of cigarette smoke. "Afternoon," said the man behind the counter, as he clumsily shoved his ashtray underneath.

"Hi. Just taking a quick browse, okay?" Desiree said.

"Sure," he hacked, his bloodshot eyes following her. She headed across the filthy floor back to an adjoining room. Dusty shelves sagged beneath piles of chipped dishes, cookie jars, and teapots. On the floor were broken bins of old Dinky toys, piggybanks and board games. A door stood ajar to a foul-smelling room where a dog snored on a dishevelled cot. She wandered back out to the main area and looked around. Flour bins, washboards, tins, jugs. She approached the counter.

"I'm actually searching for a specific item which was sold at an estate sale on the weekend of July 6 in Oyster Bay, over Westside. Would you possibly have been at that sale?"

"Ahh no," he replied, rubbing his forearm. "I don't do the buyin', and most of our stuff is donated. Whatcha' lookin' for?"

She took a final glance around the store. "Never mind. Thanks anyway," she said and, with a weak smile, quickly escaped through the broken screen door.

The man followed her outside. "You're the HungerStop lady."

Desiree stopped and turned to face him. "Yes, that's right."

"'Member me?"

"Well, now. I must say you do look a bit familiar."

With a toothless smile, he yanked up a sleeve.

"Well, of course!" she said. "How could I ever forget that tattoo!" Desiree dug deep to remember this man in more detail. The volunteer with the DESIREE tattoo. "Yes, you worked at our distribution centre in Port Sherman. So nice to see you again, and forgive me for not recognizing you." Desiree swept her gaze around the neglected property. "You left the city, I take it?"

"Yah, after I left HungerStop, I rented a travel trailer over Westside for a while. Was doing some work for the golf course."

"Oh really? Groundskeeping... that sort of thing?"

"Snorkellin' golf balls outta the bay. Took me a whole month to get 'em all. They paid me fifty cents each. Not bad, seeing how I found almost six hundred. They got the nets up now though, so I guess I won't be doin' that job no more."

"A man of many talents." Desiree laughed. "So, you're no longer living in the travel trailer in Westside?"

"Nope. Got run out of the neighbourhood."

"Oh? How did that happen?"

"A guy reported me for botherin' kids at the playground, but I was only checking the bins for recyclin'. I'd never hurt a kid. Never. But then word got around, and I didn't wanna see nobody, so I just stayed in the trailer." He drew a noxious drag from his cigarette. "Anyways, I answered the door one night and got roughed up pretty bad. Next thing ya know, the trailer's burned out. I'm doing all right now, though. I work here for nuthin' and the owner lets me and my dog, Gert, sleep out back."

"How awful!" Desiree said. "Who reported you, and where was the trailer? I mean whereabouts did you live over Westside?"

"Just up past the church."

CHAPTER 26

Desiree's second day on the road was more disappointing than the first, despite having six more antique and collectible shops now crossed off the list. She phoned Sully.

"Come with me tomorrow, will you? This is more grueling than I thought."

"Are you kidding? Spend the day prowling junk shops with my favorite girl? I'll meet you at the waterfront. Treat you to an ice cream. Around eleven?"

Desiree waited on a waterfront bench, watching in amusement as Sully struggled to parallel park her oversized Pontiac between two tour buses. Childhood memories flooded back. Sully with outstretched arms at the end of her driveway. Desiree crossing the great expanse of Austin Road. *That's a good girl. You looked both ways. Now what's that you've brought me?* Then always much ado about the *Reader's Digest* or the spool of black thread or the three teabags. There was never a Sully-man, nor any Sully-kids, but there were pansies along her walkway and peppermints in a bowl, and these things more than compensated for the shortfall.

"What kind did you get?" asked Sully as the two women sat down with their ice cream cones.

"Oh, I don't know. Tiger-Track-Dinosaur-Bones. Something like that." Desiree squinted across the bay to Westside. "You know, with the leaves on the trees, you can barely see the church steeple from here any more... which reminds me, Sully, do you know of a travel trailer that used to be over there? Near the church?"

"Oh, that's gone now. Burned. Between you and me, pretty sure Reverend Fry had a hand in that."

"Oh really? Where was it? I don't remember any trailer."

"Oh, it was just up the road from your mother's house. It was hidden in there for years. Then the property owner cut down some lilacs and folks could see it."

"And the Friar didn't like that?"

"Well, you know... a welfare bum. Unsightly premises and all that." Like a glossy earthworm embedded in the flesh, Sully's scar tugged and twisted at her mouth as she twirled her ice cream against her prickly tongue. "And we can't have that now, can we?" she said. "Not over Westside."

Desiree felt her jaw stiffen but decided to let the subject drop. She would get to the bottom of this, but for now, she mustn't ruffle the feathers of Rita Sullivan, the Friar's most loyal disciple. "Hey, what's that sign down the end of the boardwalk?" Desiree asked. "Does that say The Wharf Rat?" She pulled the rumpled yellow pages from her pocket. "It's right here on the waterfront! Bonus. We'll go there now and cross it off tomorrow's list."

The ungainly man was sweeping the floor when the two women stepped inside. Desiree quickly scanned the shelves and tabletops, glanced at Sully, and raised an optimistic eyebrow.

"G'day ladies," he said cheerily as he propped his broom against the counter.

"Good day to you!" said Desiree, and she went on to explain, once again, the nature of her quest.

The old chap tugged hard on his beard. "Well, now. Estate sale, July 6 and 7, hey? Yep, I mighta been at that one... over

Westside you say?" Desiree tried to remain calm. "Was there some old yardsticks... and ahh..." His bushy eyebrows shot skyward in recall. "And old hunting rifles?"

Desiree swallowed noisily. "Yes, yes. My father collected pretty much everything," she laughed.

A tattered binder was dragged from beneath the counter and Sully's elbow dug deeply into Desiree's ribs as the old man licked his callused thumb and began pawing at the pages. The women watched in agony as his chewed fingernails scratched, inch by stubborn inch, down the columns of inventory, then stopped. "Yup. I sold it July 11. I remember the family now. New in town. Don't know their names. They bought a bunch of stuff that day. I do see the boy around though. Can't miss him! Blue hair, heh heh. I'll see what I can find out for you, Miss. Just write down your number, right here on this pad." Then, with much bemusement, he watched the two women playfully high-five one another straight through the tinkling screen door.

***

His cloudy eyes narrowed in the afternoon sun as the boys came rumbling along the wooden boardwalk toward The Wharf Rat. "Ah. There he is," he said with satisfaction and he stepped forward. "Hey, you boy," he gestured, hand in the air. "Can you stop a minute?"

Matthew flipped his skateboard into the air and grabbed it. "Yah?"

"Ignore him," said Leevon. "Come on, dude. He's a weirdo."

Matthew looked confused. "Huh?"

Leevon lowered his voice. "He wants Mom to dress up like a rat... you know, for his Labour Day sale."

"Yah, so? Your mom does that stuff."

"Yah, but she said no, and he keeps buggin' her. I'm telling ya, man. He creeps me out. Let's go."

The man stood patiently, shielding his eyes from the sun, holding a card between two fingers.

"My mom said NO, ya creep!" Leevon hollered.

" No your friend there. I need to speak to your friend," he said.

"What for?" asked Matt.

The man limped toward them and handed Matthew his business card. "Ask your father to call me, eh?"

"My dad doesn't have a rat suit either."

"Just get him to call me, eh? Like a good lad?"

CHAPTER 27

Dan tried unsuccessfully to contact his wife and son, as his every phone call was answered by one of his in-laws, neither of whom had much to say.

"Put Karla on please, Mildred," Dan pleaded. "I need to speak to her."

"She's not available."

"Well, where's Matthew? Can I speak to him?"

"Sorry, Dan. They're not here right now."

"For God's sake, Mildred, lighten up. We've been family for years."

"Excuse me? My daughter sacrificed body, blood and soul for your parents for the past four years, so don't talk to me about happy families. Then what did YOU do for her in return? You dragged her and Matthew out to snob town and shacked them up in your little house-of-horrors."

"Mildred, you can't stop me from coming there to see them."

"Maybe not, but your father-in-law sure can. Don't poke the bear, Dan. Stay away."

He certainly didn't need the house-of-horrors jab. Unbeknownst to Mildred, unbeknownst to his father-in-law, unbeknownst to any of them, he himself had not had the courage to enter his own premises since the day Karla and Matthew fled the scene. Outdoor living had its comforts. Dan hung up the phone and was drunk before noon.

***

At the bar and grill on the waterfront, Dan pulled a stool to the outside terrace. He'd spent the afternoon snoozing off a hangover in the shade of his backyard pines, and was now craving pub grub – some well-deserved grease – and, of course, a few cold ones. With his face warmly lit by the setting sun, Dan watched as shimmering paths of pink and orange streaked across the waters of the bay. Everything was tinted orange – the gleaming fiberglass of the boats, the wispy clouds drifting overhead, even the seagulls perched atop the lamp posts. Beautiful people in storybook lives wandered throughout the cheery kiosks and ice cream stands – a veritable pageant of tanned legs, designer shades and dazzling smiles. Dan wondered if any of their stomachs felt quivery and caustic like his.

"What can I bring you this fine evening?" asked the young waitress.

"Oh! Sorry," Dan laughed. "I zoned out there for a minute there. Um, what microbrews do you have on tap?"

The ponytail, tightly gathered and secured to the crown of her head, spun like a helicopter blade as she turned her face to the chalkboard. "Garrison Red, Dark-and-Stormy, House Party, and Black Angus," she chirped.

Dan swept his hand along the bar. "Line 'em up!"

"You want a tester tray?"

"Nope! A pint of each please!"

"All four at once? They'll get warm in this heat."

"Trust me," Dan said, "they won't have time."

Dan watched from his barstool as the sun dipped below the horizon and the evening crowd began to fill the bars and eateries. Sombre groups of teenagers lingered here and there – some huddled in obscurity, others doing everything possible to be seen and heard. Dan missed Matthew.

"Something from the menu tonight, bud?" asked the food waiter.

"Heck, yah!" said Dan. "Double ch-cheeseburger platter, large fries. Hold the coleslaw."

"Anything to drink with that?"

"Yah, I'll have a Guinness. Please. Actually, make that two."

By the time Dan got to his feet and swayed to the cash to pay his bill, a blanket of darkness had settled over the bay. "You take care now," said the waitress with the helicopter hair, as Dan spilled out into the night.

The idea hadn't seemed all that outlandish at the time. Thanks to a full moon and an epic high tide, the deck of the sailboat was just a short jump down from the dock. Just a quick hop down to rest his weary head on the plush cushions of the deck loungers. From the darkened shadows at the far end of the dock, Dan could still hear the live music and laughter resounding in the distance.

What the hell!

Dan dropped two feet onto the deck of the boat. As expected, the cabin door was locked but Dan was able to peer through the window to see his life's dream on full display, eerily illuminated by the light of his dying cell phone – the narrow galley kitchen, the stainless-steel bar fridge, the bowl of fruit, the opened marine map. Fueled by reckless envy, Dan sunk into one of the loungers, and breathed the intoxicating scent of the North Atlantic deeply into his lungs, on a rare, warm and balmy night.

Ah, the Big Dipper. There it is. Always easy to find. But the little one. Damn. I can never find it. Matt can. Matt knows his stars. Oh, there's whatcha-call-him... Orion. And Cassanova, I think she's called...

Gazing upward and tilting his head from side to side, Dan watched the sky fill with blinking fairy lights, some fading from view if he peered at them too directly, some burning steadily like the eyes of angels. The yacht rocked gently in the ripples of the bay, the lapping of the water against the bow a soothing lullaby.

Dan could not be sure what actually came first – the guy's voice or the sudden kick to the ribs – as it seemed, at least in that split second, that the running shoe itself shrieked upon impact. "GET THE JESUS OFF MY BOAT!"

"Don't hurt me. Don't hurt me," Dan wailed. Curled tightly in a ball, head squeezed between his elbows, he cried. "I just fell asleep! I was just lookin' at the stars!"

"Yah? Is it stars you wanna see? Cuz I can show you some BIG mothers!" came the voice from the darkness. "Turn on the damned light, Jen!"

Dan heard the tinkle of a key followed by the squeak of the cabin door. Shielding his eyes from the sudden beam of light, Dan pleaded. "Just let me go. I never touched anything, okay?"

With both paws, the man grabbed Dan by the shirt and dragged him to his feet.

"Wait," said the woman. "I know this guy. He's no trouble. Put him down."

Dan dropped like a hot potato back onto the lounger. "What? You know this piece of shit?"

"Yes, he used to schedule our pain clinic patients," she said quietly. "We worked together. I know him well."

Dan elbowed himself to a sitting position and squinted into the light. "Doc Durling? Oh, hell no," he moaned as he hid his face in his hands. "Please, can we just forget this ever happened? I'll go quietly."

"Let me help you up," she said. Dan accepted the doctor's hand, protectively holding his ribs as he rose to his feet. "Ow! Ow!" he cried. "OW!"

"Oh, for Christ's sake," said the man.

"You smell like a brewery," she said. "You won't be driving

anywhere."

"Of course not. I'm walking. I'm not stupid."

"HA!" yelped the man. "Who's been feeding you THAT lie?"

"Can you call yourself a taxi?" she asked.

Dan pulled his phone from his pocket. "Um… no. Battery's dead."

"Okay," she said calmly, "I'll call." Humiliated, Dan avoided the man's sneer as the doctor called the taxi on her phone. "You have means to pay, right? Cash. Credit card?" she asked.

Dan suddenly started groping at his pockets. "Where's my wallet?" Dan's head spun to the lounger. Prodding between the cushions, he said, "It's gone. My wallet's gone."

"Jesus H. Christ," the man muttered.

"I must have left it at the cash register. Up there at the pub."

"George," she said, "run up and see if they have his wallet."

"ME! Why should I—"

"Just go!" she said, and her husband disappeared cursing into the night.

"Don't worry," she said. "If we can't find your wallet, I have some cash. Ace Taxi has a stand on Bayshore, just outside the parking lot. They said there'll be a car waiting."

"But I live just up the hill."

"You're unsteady on your feet. Take the ride."

George returned and shoved the wallet into Dan's tender ribs. "Anything else you need? Loser?" he sniggered.

"Actually, yah. A washroom, if you don't mind." Dan replied.

"Not on MY boat!" the man hissed. "You can damn well piss in the bay!"

Dan looked sheepishly at his former colleague. "It's okay," she said. "No one at the hospital will ever hear of this."

Dan gingerly climbed up onto the dock and headed for the taxi stand, but his evening of humiliation was far from over. Halfway up Pinehill Avenue, Dan hollered for the taxi driver to pull over. Peering at Dan in the rearview mirror, the driver said, "We're almost to your street, man. Can't it wait?"

"No! Stop!" he cried, and tumbled out the back door. After relieving himself on the side of the road, Dan slumped back into the taxi and, in a matter of minutes, they turned into his driveway.

"What do I owe ya?" Dan asked, picking at his wallet.

"Nothing, we're good," the driver replied.

"Huh? How come?" asked Dan, as he tried passing a twenty over the seat.

"I said NO! I don't want your money. Now get out."

Confused, Dan obeyed the order and stood watching in the driveway, as the driver stepped out of the taxi with a squirt bottle and, with a look of disgust, sanitized the backdoor handles inside and out, sanitized the backseat, sanitized his hands, climbed back in and drove away.

Dan shoved the twenty back into his wallet and collapsed on the back step.

ASSHOLE! IDIOT! You couldn't crash on a stranger's boat, could you? No, not you. So listen up, dummy. You're pulling yourself together right here and now. You're going inside the house. Yup. Tonight.

A thunderous belch of stale beer and raw onions rang out in the night.

Well, maybe just take a look in the living room window first. After a cigarette. And a swig of Captain. No rush. Hey, where did the stars go? The sky was full of them earlier... on the boat. Doc Durling's boat. You'd screw up a Sunday school picnic given half the chance.

A moody and darkened moon lurked behind shifting clouds,

and a clammy draft of air breathed at the back of Dan's neck. He flicked his cigarette butt across the lawn, grabbed a stinking hoodie from the trunk of the car, pulled it on, zipped it up. He then slid the hidden rum bottle from under the picnic table and, gripping it by the neck, groped along the gravel footpath to the front of the house. The rhododendron bushes waited in ambush around the corner, first hidden in the shadows, then leaning into his path, misshapen and silent. Dan stopped, disoriented, cowering from the bushes. With shallow and ragged breaths, he yanked up his hood and took an uneasy gulp from the bottle. All that was left of the moon was a yellowish smudge on the sky. Spitting rain had begun to fall. Just a few more steps to the front door. Dan turned to the verandah and began to climb the stairs. A hanging spider web attached itself and stretched across his lips. Revolted, he spat, and wiped it away on his sleeve. He reached the top step. On shaky legs, he steadied himself against the railing and, with eyes closed, slowly lifted his face to the living room window.

Go ahead and look. Chickenshit.

Blood beat painfully in Dan's ears as he suddenly turned away and sucked the bottle dry. The empty bottle dropped to the verandah boards and rolled away.

Come on, you coward.

Dan gripped the railing with both hands, blew out an unsteady breath, and raised his eyes to the glass. And there it was. Hovering over the fireplace, an orb breathing an eerie green light. Inhaling, exhaling. Pulsating bright, brighter, then dim. Growing in size and intensity, then shrinking away. Ghostly images crawled along the walls, snaked across the floor, reached through the rain-spattered window. Dan froze. Mesmerized, he gaped through the glass until a whine, like the whimper of a baby, found its way to his lips. Then, with an agonizing wail, Dan twisted away, but his two feet remained planted in place. Terrified, he collapsed in a heap, rolled down the stairs, and fled to the sanctity of his backyard. After several hours of sitting upright in his vehicle – its high beams illuminating the entire property – Dan fell into a troubled sleep.

CHAPTER 28

Days passed. Dan slept in his car in the driveway, urinated on the compost pile or used public facilities when the specific need arose. Devouring fast food on the patio, he tossed his empty bottles into the outside bin. Embarrassed and ashamed. Afraid to enter his own house. Too drunk to move. Too sick to care. Slumped in a lawn chair, he felt another empty bottle slip through his fingers, heard it tinkle across the flagstones. Offending odours escaped his clothing with every bodily shift.

When the hell was my last shower... the day she left... the day before...

Dan squinted through bloodshot eyes across the lawn, as the curious round red object came into focus.

What the... aw, shit! Our first tomato.

What a fun day this might have been. The red acidic juice would drip from Karla's chin, and they would both laugh, or high-five. Maybe even hug.

Hey, you. Sunflowers. Don't hang your heads. She never liked me either.

Drifting off again, disturbing images flitted throughout his dreams. Lucy Halliburton slashing a razor blade through a juicy red tomato. Lucy Halliburton scattering colourful pills across the floor. A swollen face spinning in a noose. Dan awoke with a start. Branded with the imprint of the plastic lawn chair across his sweaty back, he sat forward.

Aw, no. Not again.

He dropped his hand to his crotch. It was dry. His pants were vibrating, that's all. Something in the pocket. He twisted himself from the chair and clawed at his phone. A jackhammer pounded behind his eyes.

"Karla? Zat you?"

Her tone was icy. "What am I interrupting? Another date with the Captain?"

"Jussa a few drinks in the… in the sun, that's all. I miss you… and Matty. How's my little buddy, Matty? I wanna be with you guys. My two best buddies."

"Pity's sake, Dan. Get a grip. I'm expecting something in the mail. Work related. Brown government envelope. Have you seen it? It's important."

"The mail? From the… from the mailbox?"

"Yah, you know, the metal box with the name DUGGAN at the end of the driveway. Oh my God!"

His head spun like a roulette wheel. Dan couldn't recall at that moment just exactly where the driveway was located, let alone the mailbox. "When can I come there, be with you guys?"

"Whenever hell freezes over. The envelope?"

Struggling to a standing position, Dan took a sip of stale warm water and staggered to the shade. "If I come to Port Sherman, can we be together? Like before?"

"What do you mean like before? In Mom and Dad's basement apartment? Think again. They don't want you here."

"What about all your stuff, hmmm? All Matty's, Matty's st-stuff?" he asked, hiccups jolting his every word.

Silence.

"Karla? Whud we gonna do?" His voice was thick with emotion.

"You figure it out," she said and hung up.

"Can I talk to my Matty?"

Dan stared dumbly at the *Call Ended* message, slung his phone across the patio table, and leaned heavily on his knuckles amid the clutter. His legs wobbled and trembled beneath him as he began to salivate with an all-too-familiar queasiness rising in his belly. Stumbling toward the bushes, his stomach contents splashed out in a wide swath before him. He dragged his grimy forearm across his lips and tried to recall what he had eaten earlier, but the answer would be forever lost in the brown goo now dripping through Karla's roses. That night, Dan pulled his smelly sleeping bag over his head in the backseat of the car, and angrily punched at the cushion under his neck. *"YOU figure it out. Loser. YOU figure it out,"* the voices taunted.

CHAPTER 29

As the dog days of summer continued to pass, Dan became increasingly powerless to distinguish one day from another. Days from nights. Dreams from reality. Running his tongue over fuzzy teeth, he slumped barefoot against his back door. Rare moments of clarity appeared before his eyes, then vanished. Snippets of conversations with familiar faces left him baffled and disturbed. A car door slammed. He lifted gummy eyes to the police cruiser parked in the driveway.

What the…

A uniformed officer stepped onto the lawn and casually strolled toward him. "Morning, Mr. Duggan. Mighty fine tomato you got there," he said gazing at the vine. "So ripe it's about to burst."

"The only one that grew," Dan said. "Are my wife and boy all right?"

The police officer raised an eyebrow. "Your wife and boy? You got reason to believe they are not all right?"

"No, no. I just… don't know why… you know… why you're here." Dan glanced about his littered yard in embarrassment, then suddenly jerked his gaze to his car. "I wasn't driving, was I?"

The officer offered a rueful smile. "Thankfully, no, and the people of Oyster Bay can kiss the ground for that small favour. I brought you home last night."

Squinting and holding a shaky hand to his eyes, Dan ventured into the painful unknown. "What did I do, then?"

"You don't remember that open bottle of Captain Morgan sloshing around in your pocket yesterday?"

Dan drew a blank. "My pocket?"

"Down the waterfront."

Dan dropped his head and rubbed his temples. "I dunno. I dunno. Don't remember any bottle. Don't remember anything."

"Well, now, is that a fact. Because the stock clerk at the liquor store sure as heck remembers. You cracked the seal right there in the store and poured half of it down your neck. Then you shoved it in your pocket and escaped through the rotating door. It's all on camera."

Dan dropped his face into his hands.

The rotating door. Oh Gawd. Yah, it was hot. Kids were pointing. Pointing and laughing.

The officer folded his arms across his burly chest and glanced around the yard. "You spend a lot of time outside here, do ya?"

"Yup. Yup, I do."

"Want me to take a look around inside?"

"No."

"You sure? Because last night in the squad car, you were quite convinced something's in there. A ghost or something, messing with your porch light?"

"Huh? Oh, no. I mean, a few nights ago, I was sitting at the picnic table there having a smoke and watching the moths around the bulb, and then boom, everything went black. Kinda freaked me out, that's all."

"Where's the switch?"

"Inside the door. To the left."

The officer navigated around Dan, opened the door, stepped inside and flicked the switch. "The bulb's burned out," he said.

"They tend to do that, you know, when they're left on all summer."

"Oh," said Dan. "Okay."

"And guess what?"

"What."

"Not a ghost or goblin in sight," he said. "Look, Mr. Duggan, you need to get a hold-a yourself, okay?"

"Yup."

"You're a lucky man," the cop said. "The liquor store's not pressing charges. They say you're a regular customer and a decent guy. And look, I don't know what's going on with you and the family, but it appears you got some serious issues goin' on, know what I mean? Straighten yourself out. I'm gonna keep an eyeball peeled on you, and I don't ever want a repeat of yesterday, understand?"

Dan rose and extended his hand. Hanging his head in shame, he managed, "Thanks for bringing my sorry ass home last night. I'll settle up with the liquor store."

The police officer returned to his cruiser, slid into the driver's seat and hollered through the open window, "Oh, and that busload of cheerleaders..."

An anguished moan escaped Dan's throat. "What cheerlea..." his voice trailed off.

The cop flashed a toothy grin. "They figure for a guy your age, you really got the moves!" As the cruiser pulled away, taunting visions of blue and white pompoms drifted across Dan's consciousness.

Go, Dan! Go, Dan! G-o-o-o, DAN!

Dan pinched a cigarette butt from the pocket of his sweat pants, teased it into the shape of a garden slug and lit it. With three deep sucks, he gave his lungs the morning scorch they craved. He then sloshed his hand through the warm waters of the picnic cooler and plucked out the last bottle of beer. Skunky, sure, but it delivered the desired effect, and Dan was able to find his way to Hava Java for his morning jolt of caffeine. "Morning, bud!" hollered the young man at the coffee urn. "The usual?"

"Might try a large Colombian this morning! And one of those badass blueberry muffins." Dan laughed. He then spent the next half hour blissfully sipping strong black coffee, gnawing at his muffin, fully absorbed in the Bay Bulletin. But when he left the table to make his way to the washroom, Dan with his rolled-up towel and kit bag caught the manager's attention. He blocked Dan's path. "Excuse me, sir," the man said. "I'm afraid I can no longer allow you to use our facilities for personal hygiene purposes."

"Huh?" Dan glanced around the shop. "How come? I bought a coffee and muffin. I always buy a coffee and muffin. I come here every morning."

"Sir, you've been reported for shaving, shampooing your hair, and brushing your teeth in there."

"So? It's a washroom."

"I'm going to have to ask you to leave."

Dan jammed his towel under an armpit. "Who reported me?" he demanded, looking furiously around the cafe. His friendly coffee boy stood behind the cash register. "Was it him?" he asked.

"NO!" said the manager. "A few customers complained. Now, it's time to leave," he said. "I don't want any trouble."

Dan's cheeks were ablaze. Angry and humiliated, he stormed out of his favorite hangout without so much as paying.

CHAPTER 30

A week passed, and Hava Java wasn't the only local business to have put the run to Dan and his morning rituals. Now barred from the washrooms at both the Irving Gas Stop and the Atlantic Superstore, Dan grimaced behind the steering wheel on Route 14 at the campground gates. It was ten thirty a.m.

I need a toilet, and I need one now.

He pulled into the campground. Beyond the gates, Gem maneuvred a roaring lawnmower around a plank picnic table. Dan grabbed his kit bag and slid gingerly from the car. "Hey, Gem!" he hollered. Squeezing his buttocks around the automatic gate post, he tried again. "MORNING, GEM!"

Gem dug the plugs from her ears and turned off the mower. "Oh. Hi, Dan," she said, peering behind him at his hastily parked car. "What brings you here this morning?"

"Oh nothing… I mean, um…" Dan jammed his kit bag under an arm.

Gem loosened her grip on the mower and squinted in the sun. "You okay?"

Dan's eyes darted to the washrooms. "I… ah." He jerked his head in their direction.

"Oh!" Gem laughed. "Taken short on the highway, were you?"

"May I?" he asked.

"Of course!" she said. "Go, go. Hurry, hurry!" Gem's infectious giggle followed him all the way to the washroom door.

Twenty minutes later, emerging from the facilities with bowels purged, teeth brushed and whiskers shaved, Dan tried to slip away. Gem again turned off the mower.

"I'm so embarrassed," said Dan.

"Ach! Don't be silly," she teased. "Time for my tea break. Join me?"

"Um, yah. Why not?" said Dan, and he followed her to the motor home.

"So, Dan," Gem said as she placed a tray on her outside patio table, "I don't mean to pry. I just want to know how Matthew's doing at his grandparents' place in Port Sherman. Leevon's like a lost puppy around here."

"He's doing okay. I guess," Dan said. "I don't speak to him much."

After a pause of awkward silence, Gem changed tack. "Say!" she said cheerily, "anytime you want to come for a swim, the pool is pretty much empty on weekday mornings."

Are you kidding me right now? Did she really just say that? That would kick the hell out of my washroom wipe-downs.

"It's beautifully refreshing," Gem said. "Saltwater. Pumped in from the ocean and solar heated."

Dan regarded the bank of solar panels. "Wow, heated and all, eh? Would the campground owner object? I'm not a camper, you know, like a paying customer."

"He lets me bend the rules for a few friends, especially during downtimes."

Dan emptied his mug with a loud slurp, and turned his gaze to the pool sparkling in the morning sun, tranquil and inviting. "I just might take you up on that, Gem! Right now!" he said. "I just need to get a couple things from the car. Is that okay?"

"Sure. It's gonna be a scorcher," she said. "Give me a minute to open the gate." Gem disappeared inside for a few seconds and returned. "Okay, bring your car in," she said, "and enjoy your dip, Dan." Gem twisted the plugs back into her ears, and gave the mower cord two or three hard yanks, and was off.

Dan flipped the trunk lid and rummaged through the twisted pile of dirty clothes, blankets, pillows, soggy washcloths and towels. After a pair of musty swimming trunks was flung free of the mess, he reached into the wheel jack compartment and slid out a pint of dark rum. In the changing room, he shoved the bottle into his trunks, stepped out into the blazing sun and slid into the shallow end. Paradise.

It was noon before Dan thrust himself up the rungs of the ladder to the pool deck, and clumsily wrapped the empty bottle in his towel. "Thanks, Gem! That was AMAZING!" he shouted, waving across the campground lawns, grinning like a Cheshire cat. "Can I come again tomorrow?" Leevon watched him skeptically from the doorway of the motor home. Gem offered a half-hearted thumbs-up in his general direction. Whatever. In Dan's mind, that was a clear sign of agreement, and he happily drove home well over the blood alcohol limit. Once in the privacy of his backyard, he peeled off his shirt and slumped down in a plastic lawn chair. White saltwater residue crusted in the crevices of his skin. "Oh Captain, my Captain," he sighed as he broke the seal on a shiny new bottle. The amber liquid burned its way to his empty belly and yet another summer afternoon was swallowed up in the black hole of his senses.

***

"Hey! Mr. Duggan." Someone was shaking his wrist.

"Leave him alone," a voice said. "Let's go."

"We're friends of Matt's. Wake up."

Dan's eyes shot open to the sky. "Is Matty okay?"

"Yah, mister. He's cool. Far as we know."

"Well then, scram."

"You're blistering, dude. Get outta the sun. Get up."

The boys pulled Dan to his feet and dragged him to the shade. "Let's get you inside. You need a cold shower or somethin'. You're purple, man." With his tongue plastered to the roof of his mouth, Dan managed to mutter, "Bottled water in the trunk." The boys returned with the entire carton of twenty-four. Dan guzzled one, twisted the cap from a second, and poured it over his chest and knees. "I'll be all right, guys," he said sheepishly. "Matt's not around. So how come you're here?"

"Delivering flyers," one said. "Heard you snoring."

"Oh, okay. Well, thanks for the wake-up call, to excuse the pun," he said with a feeble smile. "Appreciate it. I'll be all right. You boys be on your way, now. Go on." Later that night, in the backseat of the car, Dan squirmed without clothing and without covers as the skin of his torso lifted in angry, punishing blisters.

***

Dan tumbled out onto the warm asphalt of his driveway and struggled to a standing position. Propping himself on the open car door, he noisily expelled his morning phlegm and padded barefoot to the compost pile. Upon relieving himself, he zipped his fly and gazed about the yard. Chickadees flitted happily through the pines. Yesterday's flyers lay undisturbed in their plastic sleeve. Captain Morgan, foot hitched on a barrel, sneered at him from an empty bottle on the lawn. The solitary tomato, having lost its grip on the vine, sat mushy on the soil. Dan gravitated toward the garden. Dropping to his knees, he gently scooped the tomato from the earth. Cavities of decay blemished its once glossy skin, and the burst of a fleshy wound laid bare its inner pulp. The muscles of Dan's chin began to tremble. Red hot tears fell from his eyes, onto the forsaken fruit, through his open fingers and into the soil. Dan remained crouched in the garden until the waves of nausea, shame and guilt subsided, his shoulders stopped shaking, and his tears dried in salty smudges on his face. Dan rolled first onto his side, then onto his back in the cool grass. His respirations steadied. Wispy clouds drifted high above the pine trees. The pale crescent of the morning moon hung silently in the western sky. The silver speck of a passenger jet streaked a foamy path overhead, as the thinning remains of earlier flights, tinged with the pink of the rising sun, dissipated into the blue. He heard not a sound. Not a bird nor passing vehicle. Not a yapping dog nor slamming door. Dan felt his limbs relax. His jaw. His scalp. Gazing into the heavens, he no longer felt the prickle of the grass beneath. No longer felt the fire in his scorched skin, nor the twist of anxiety in his belly. A sense of ease spread throughout his mind and body, flooding his limbs. He bent to a sitting position. An unfamiliar force surged in his chest, gaining strength as it lifted him from the earth. Singing. Breathing. As surely as the sun rose over the Bay, Dan's moment of truth had come. As clearly as a mountain stream it flowed, and with the power of a raging fire, it burned. He rose to his feet.

This is it. Now or never. Do or die.

CHAPTER 31

Dan teetered his way to the patio table and began dropping items of rubbish into a garbage bag. Then, with an impatient and indiscriminate sweep of his arm across the table, everything tumbled into the bag – sleeping pills, fast food wrappers, cigarette butts, dirty socks, crushed beer cans – leaving nothing behind but a few smudges of ketchup and dried bird droppings.

The ball was in his court. Karla had made that painfully clear and, as the morning dew glistened on the shaggy lawn, Dan swore off alcohol. Rum, wine and beer bottles, sticky and stinking in the August sun, fell into recycling bags. Blankets, pillows, and heaps of dirty clothes hauled from the backseat of the car, coffee cups, creamers and napkins swept from the front.

The tiny Cape Cod was oppressive with dead air as Dan ventured inside. Karla's Harlequin novel, *Into the Abyss*, lay beside the coffee pot wherein blotches of green mold floated on a blackened slurry. Matthew's backpack lay slung across the table, and the radio was quietly emitting the CKJN Morning News. Dan stopped in his tracks.

Wait. She left in a hurry. So who turned on the radio? Don't run. Deep breaths. Think. Oh yah, it was me. I made coffee, then I got drunk. Pretty sure…

In the kitchen, Dan twisted the sink faucet. His heart leaped as the water pump groaned and shuddered. Water, brown and stinky, sputtered into the sink. Allowing the water to run clear, he tiptoed into the living room. Houseflies buzzed and bounced against the windows. On the coffee table, two wine glasses stood side by side, their contents half evaporated - a jolting and painful reminder of the quarrel with his wife – when she'd pleaded with him to listen. Just listen. Tiny specks of a hundred dead fruit flies floated on the red scum. Karla's haphazard cosmetic bag, having slipped from her grasp in her hasty departure, lay unzipped on the floor. Lipsticks, hairclips and cough drops lay strewn in all directions. Pulse pounding in his ears, Dan forced his gaze to the fireplace hearth and, to his wonder, nothing menacing to behold. Bricks and mortar and the usual grey dust. Objects on the mantle lay silent and undisturbed, alongside Karla's fully charged camera battery, harmlessly blinking its green light.

Oh my God. You dummy!

Dan blew a breath of relief and began to shake off the jitters. He returned to the sink and turned off the faucet, climbed the creaking staircase, showered and straightened the bedroom. Braved the basement laundry and washed the twisted mess of damp and smelly items from the car trunk. Hung them on the clothesline. Scrubbed and swept, cleaned out the refrigerator, and while dumping a container of curdled milk, was suddenly blindsided by his first craving of the day. Overcome with dizzying thoughts of alcohol, tobacco, weed, anything, everything, he headed for the grocery store, altering his route to avoid the liquor store. He'd pay for the bottle of Captain another day. With cravings pecking and drilling at his nerves, Dan stalked the aisles, hands trembling in evidence of an addiction he only dimly realized. He filled his cart with bottled water, fresh fruit and produce, and returned home to prepare his first nutritious meal in weeks. After a tossed green salad with cold ham and French bread, Dan brewed a pot of strong black tea. Having survived his first day of sobriety, he headed upstairs with the folded laundry. "I'll figure it out, all right," he bellowed out the upstairs window. "OH YAH, I'LL FIGURE IT THE HELL OUT!"

***

Two days passed. With the property now completely cleared of rubbish, Dan rolled the lawnmower from the shed. The ankle-high grass was still damp with morning dew but the sun shone brilliantly, and Dan had more energy than he'd felt in weeks. Months. A quick top-up of gasoline and a few good yanks on the cord, and Dan was roaring about the yard in diagonal lines, throwing grass clippings into sodden rows with each pass. The rake and wheelbarrow were the next to see the light of day, and by lunch time, the Duggan property looked respectable again. The thistles and chickweed choking the flower gardens could wait another day.

Dan slid an ice-cold bottle of spring water from the refrigerator and guzzled it dry. The Wharf Rat business card lay undisturbed on the kitchen table where Matt had tossed it weeks before. A lifetime before. Dan frowned at Matt's handwritten scrawl across the card. "Dad, call this guy".

What could that old fella possibly want from me. If I could just speak to Matthew, I'd know. Oh, well, what the hell.

Dan picked up the phone and dialled the number. "Hello. Dan Duggan here. My son says you wanted me to call?"

The old man cleared his throat. "Ah... oh yes! I thought perhaps the boy forgot. Dan, is it? Duggan you say?"

"That's right."

"Dan. Duggan. Good... you see, there was a nice lady come in a few weeks ago. I had picked up a few pieces from her mother's estate over Westside, and one of them things, well... she needs it back. Now, if my memory serves, you bought some of that stuff from me. I remember you coming in early summer, you and your family, and I seen your boy a few times after that on the wharf. I got the lady's number here. She'd be mighty pleased if you gave her a ring."

Dan glanced around the living room, at the ship's lantern, the duck decoy, the brass candlesticks. The ugly driftwood picture frame. "Yah, okay, why not," he sighed, and jotted down her number.

"Like I said, she'd be awful pleased. Real nice lady."

When Desiree answered the phone, she was excited, exhilarated, pleading and apologetic. "Please, Mr. Duggan, I beg of you. May I come to see the items you purchased the Wharf Rat? I do apologize for this imposition, but please. It means the world to me."

"Yah? The whole world?"

"I live in Port Sherman. I can be there within the hour."

"You wanna come today?" he whined. NASCAR was about to start.

"Please."

"131 Pinehill Avenue, corner of Jeffries"he moaned, and climbed upstairs to his toothbrush.

When the knock came to the back door, Dan pushed the screen door open, forcing Desiree to step back. "You found the place!" He flashed her his infamous, gleaming smile but telltale lines of strain and fatigue crinkled at the corners of his eyes. His bare feet were tanned and sinewy. The kitchen smelled of fried onions. The TV was blaring.

"Very sorry to trouble you," she said as she fiddled with her purse. Dan held open the door as she stepped inside.

She extended her hand. "I'm Desiree MacLeod. I do appreciate this. I've been searching for weeks. I know this must all seem quite bizarre."

With a hint of sarcasm and a challenging grin, Dan pointed through the screen door to the yard. "Is it the lobster trap out there?"

"No," Desiree managed a weak smile. "Not the lobster trap."

"How about those glass buoys out there, hanging on the shed?"

"No, not those."

"Follow me," he said, as he led Desiree through the kitchen to the living room. He hit the mute button on the TV, and casually swept the back of his hand about the room. "So. See it anywhere?" Desiree stood motionless in the doorway. "Well?" Dan asked. Her head moved not a fraction, but her eyes slowly surveyed every object in the room. Dan waited. "Are you always this mysterious?" he asked in a slightly mocking tone. Desiree remained silent – her gaze finally fixing to the fireplace mantle. Dan moved in front of her. "Look, lady, if you're just gonna stand there, I have better things…"

"Please," she said quietly. "You're standing in my way."

"Well, pardon me all to hell!" he laughed, but again he stood aside.

Desiree grasped the back of the armchair to maintain her balance, then took an unsteady step toward the fireplace. "May I?"

"May you what?"

"See the decoy."

"So that's your holy grail?"

"Yes." Desiree lifted the decoy from the mantle and cradled it in her arms. "The King," she whispered.

"Hey. You really know your ducks. You're correct. It's a King Eider."

Desiree stood transfixed, gently stroking the decoy from its head to its tail.

"Righty then!" Dan said, guiding her in the direction of the kitchen. "Glad you found it. I don't remember what I paid for it, but just take it, okay?" His eyes darted to the muted NASCAR race. Desiree stopped at the armchair and turned the decoy upside down. Squinting, she inspected her mother's handiwork. The thin, broken bead of glue no longer held the keel securely in place and, with a gentle push of her thumb, the keel dropped into the palm of her hand. Dan stepped toward her. "Now look what you did! You broke the damned thing," he said. But his words were cut short when a twisting grey cloud drifted upward from a drilled hole in the bottom of the decoy. The room grew icy cold as the cloud rose to the ceiling. Dan and Desiree stood frozen, gripped in fear, as it spread out overhead. An eerie hush fell over the room, and a dry acrid odour hung in the air. Then, in columns of pale sunlight, softly and silently to the floor, fell the ashes of Archie MacLeod.

CHAPTER 32

Swept clean of disturbing memories and broken dreams, the tiny Cape Cod sat empty on its deserted property. As Dan backed out of the driveway, he shot it one last glance, at the FOR SALE sign, the mossy stone chimney, the withered petunia reaching its spidery arms through the lobster trap in a desperate attempt to escape the premises. He gave the gearshift a brutal shove and rumbled the rented cube van down Pinehill Avenue.

The old Cranberry Bog Motel, a half kilometer down Route 14, had been recently remodeled as a rental property. Walls had been knocked out between units, creating spacious apartments, each with two picture windows overlooking the Bay. *Upscale Rental Properties, a short walk from Town Centre* the advertisement had read. Dan stepped inside. The place smelled of fresh paint and new carpet. He imagined Karla's reaction to the light and airy open concept. He envisioned Matthew, a short walk from the campground, knocking around with Leevon again. He sucked in a deep breath and with a grunt, tugged the first box off the van.

Please, Karla. I'm figuring it out. Give me another shot.

Dan pushed, pulled, yanked and dragged until the apartment was piled high with boxes. He'd ignored the cell phone call that had vibrated in his pocket, but now checked it for messages. To his shock, it was Desiree MacLeod. "Mr. Duggan. Sorry to bother you, but I think I owe you an explanation of what happened in your living room a few weeks ago. It may help you to know the whole story, my father's ashes, the decoy, everything. You must feel very unsettled. Can we get together for a chat? Coffee at the Hava Java?" Dan's knee-jerk reaction was one of contempt, for both Desiree MacLeod and for the Hava Java. But he did, admittedly, feel a certain curiosity about the decoy, and he had, after all, gone back and paid for that last coffee and muffin, so felt entitled to darken their door again. He returned Desiree's call.

***

Desiree couldn't help but notice the strain in his features when Dan entered the coffee shop, the tension in his jaw, the crumpled baggy shorts.

"First of all, call me Dan," he said, as he approached the table. "I didn't recognize you at first. You changed your hair."

Desiree fussed and fiddled with the bulging backpack hanging on the back of her seat. "Yes, I do that quite often," she smiled. "Call me Desi. Thanks for coming, Dan, and for helping me sweep up that day. I've since had a professional woodworker secure the keel back in place. Let's just say Dad won't be escaping his urn a second time."

Dan frowned and pulled her seat out from the table.

"Sorry, that was crass," she said as they both wiggled into their seats. "You doing okay?"

Dan rubbed his sweaty palms on his knees. "Yah, yah. I'll live. Selling the house."

"Well, Dan, as I said, some explanation may help you understand, maybe even close a door on this nightmare for you. I'm assuming, since you agreed to meet, you feel the same?"

"Go on."

Desiree cleared her throat. "It all started about seven years ago. My father, Archie MacLeod, was a weather technician with the Department of Environment. He developed those radiosondes, you know, the sensors they release into the atmosphere out on Baggs Island? They send them up on hydrogen-filled weather balloons to collect meteorological data."

"Baggs Island?"

"Yes, it's located off the coast of Maine, but within Canadian territorial waters."

"Got it."

"So the time had come to upgrade the transmitters, and Dad was chomping to get back out there. At that time, Baggs was home to five technicians and biologists, and Dad had come to know them quite personally. Since this would be his last visit before retirement, it was, you know, quite an emotional trip for him."

"Okay," said Dan, puzzled.

"Dad was obsessed with the island. The wind, the surf, the sand... all of it. Anyway, it was on one of his morning walks that he found the decoy. It was lying on its side at the highwater mark. He spotted its black eye peering out from beneath the seaweed and other beach debris. Now, you have to know my dad. He was a collector of all things, so imagine his excitement. He knew he had found something... possibly quite valuable."

Dan recalled his conversation with the man at The Wharf Rat. "Right. Those old hunting decoys sell for hundreds."

"Or thousands! So anyway, its paint was chipped and faded, but the unique shape and colors of its bill suggested the decoy was carved to resemble the King Eider – Dad's all-time favorite seabird!"

"Talk about a retirement gift."

"I know." Desiree smiled. "King Eiders breed in areas north

of the Arctic circle, and were aggressively hunted in the north. Dad was an avid duck hunter, so he knew something of the trade, and how lucrative it was in the '40s and '50s. Most of these gunning decoys were carved from black spruce, so obviously south of the timberline." Desiree paused and gazed out the window, then returned her eyes to Dan's. "Anyway, he carried the decoy back to his lab on the island and, after studying his map of ocean currents, decided that it was most likely set adrift somewhere quite far north of here, eventually finding its way south to Baggs Island on the Labrador Current."

Dan squirmed impatiently in his chair. "And?"

"Dad was like a big kid when he got home. Mom and I met him at the door. She said 'How was your last trip to your magical island, my dear? Can you retire in peace now?' Well, you should have seen the excitement on his face. 'Great!' he said. 'Job completed, mission accomplished, and a dream come true! Look what I found on the beach!' He was grinning ear to ear when he pulled it from his knapsack. 'I found THE KING!' I swear to God, Dan, he had tears in his eyes."

"Your dad sounds like quite the guy."

Desiree wiped a coffee ring from the table. "Oh, Dad had his faults, but yah, he was quite a character. Anyway, Mom wouldn't allow any more of his junk around the house, so he took the decoy downstairs to his workshop and a few days later, when the wood dried out, the bottom piece – the keel – it fell off." She tapped down her empty cup and leaned back in her chair.

Dan sat expressionless. "That's it?"

"Well, that's the decoy part of the story. I wanted you to understand my dad, and his special connection to the King."

Dan frowned and shook his head. "I'm sorry, Desiree. You'll have to move this along... I—"

"Oh, there's more, lots more, but do you want to hear it?" She peered into his empty cup. "Refill?"

Dan was now quite intrigued and feeling lighter in a weird and comfortable way. "No more coffee, but keep talking."

"All right. Dad died June of last year, then my mother died early this summer, barely a year apart." Desiree pulled a folded paper from her purse. "Mom left this note for her best friend, Sully. We didn't find it until a couple of weeks ago."

Dan hesitantly reached across the table and took the note.

"My dearest Sully," it read. *"I hope you have found this in time. In case I should die suddenly, there is something I need to confess. After Archie died, I did something he had absolutely forbidden. As you know, he's always been terribly opposed to a person's ashes being 'displayed on a shelf' to use his exact words. Undignified and barbaric, he always said. I, on the other hand, feel that being swallowed up in the cold ground is undignified and barbaric. But he scrimped and saved and bought that double cemetery plot to ensure our ashes 'proper burials'. Perish the thought. Oh Sully, I took things into my own hands, but I think Archie will forgive me. He is resting inside the King on the shelf beside my bed. Please keep him safe from harm. With much love, your friend, Alice.*

Dan looked up, puzzled. "So. Your dad's ashes sat in your mother's bedroom for a year and nobody knew? Not even you?"

"That's right. Inside the flipping duck. Then someone bought it at the estate sale."

Dan shook his head in confusion. "But where did YOU think your dad's ashes were?"

"In the ground. Another story, another time," she said, glancing at her watch. "Right now, I need to get going."

Dan struggled to digest the information. "But how did you

track it down at The Wharf Rat?" He leaned in close across the table and searched Desiree's face.

"One junk shop at a time," she said.

"Whoa. You've been one busy lady."

"Yes," Desiree laughed, as she rose from the table. "And it seems you and I have been on a collision course all summer long!"

***

Desiree left Hava Java, checked her watch, and hurried along to Captain Harry's Whale Watching Adventures. Her backpack dangled from her elbow as the captain helped her aboard the Cape Islander.

"Thank you," she said with a grin. "May I call you Harry?"

"Anything but Mary," he said. "Welcome aboard."

"Should I sit just anywhere?"

"Yep, anywhere, and feel free to move around, take pictures or whatever." Captain Harry glanced at his clipboard. *Desiree MacLeod, Private Charter $600. Paid in full.* Squinting in the sun, he scanned his eyes along the dock. "When's the rest coming?" he asked.

"Oh, it's just me, but you'll find I won't cause any trouble," she joked.

Captain Harry cleared his throat. "Just that I normally have fifteen whale watchers on board this vessel… not complaining, mind you. Just curious."

"Oh, I'm not here for the whales. The cruise is two hours, right?"

"Give or take."

"Okay, so take me straight out for the first hour, and then I'll be ready to return."

Harry pulled nervously at his suspenders. "So, no whales, no fishing, only a cruise?"

"Perfect," she smiled.

The Cape Islander motored through the mouth of Oyster Bay on a clear, cool August morning. Desiree settled comfortably on the bench seat across the stern, and turned her face to the wind. She was thankful she'd dressed in layers. As they cleared the point, the ocean swells rose up to meet them. The loud thrum of the inboard diesel was comforting as it vibrated below, and she pulled her hood tight to her face. Town Centre was growing faint in the distance. Inside the cabin, Captain Harry was at the wheel and he hollered back over his shoulder.

"Lifejackets are under the seats! Some folks wear them just to keep warm!"

"I'm fine for now, but thanks!!" The captain was obviously quite skilled at navigating the rolling ocean swells, and Desiree felt safe in his hands.

She better not be planning something stupid. No binoculars. No camera. No lifejacket. I never had a jumper on board before. But who would pay $600 to jump off a boat... then again... she'd have no use for the money after the deed was done. Jesus, I need to retire.

Desiree was lost in thought when Harry cut the engine and stepped out into the sun. Squawking seagulls seemed to appear from nowhere as the wake stopped churning.

"First hour's up!" he announced.

"Already. Okay, thanks, Harry. A bit of privacy please?"

Harry remained silent, thoughts racing. He returned to the cabin, eyes darting first to the life ring, then to the two-way radio. Keeping his headset near at hand, Harry twisted the lid from his thermos. Seagulls hovered and glided in the air currents overhead as Desiree reached into her backpack, leaned over the side and with both hands let the King slip through her fingers. She smiled as it plunged under the surface and, true to its construction, bobbed to its upright position. With salt spray in her eyes, Desiree watched it grow smaller and smaller, bobbing southbound on the Labrador Current. "You're not on a shelf anymore, Dad. Go in peace. Find yourself another windswept beach," she whispered, and she watched for several minutes until it was out of sight. Desiree shouted into the cabin. "I'm good to go now, Harry!"

"Sounds awful good to me," he said and throttled up the engine. The seagulls quickly lost interest in the unidentified bobbing object.

Whatever it was she dumped over, it sure as hell ain't edible.

Back at the wharf, Captain Harry was still scratching his head in puzzlement as he helped Desiree to the ladder. "Now you can change your sign," she chirped.

"You reckon? Change it to what?" he laughed nervously.

"Captain Harry's Whale Watching and Ocean Burials."

CHAPTER 33

The school year was about to begin and the new apartment was ready for Duggan family life. All it needed was a family. Karla had not yet decided if she and Matthew would return to Oyster Bay, and Dan was giving her the time she needed while he feathered the nest. It had taken him the best part of a week, but all crates were now unpacked, furniture carefully placed, kitchen cupboards stocked, Matthew's winter clothes hanging in his closet, Karla's Harlequin romances lined up on the bookshelf. Feeling optimistic and invigorated on his twenty-sixth day of sobriety, Dan set out for his morning run. A quick sprint out Route 14 as far as the campground, and back along Bayshore Drive to Town Centre was an easy six kilometers. Longer distances could wait for cooler temperatures.

The bay was smooth as a satin sheet when Dan collapsed on a bench at the water's edge. A thick white mist rose leisurely over the water like a stage curtain, revealing one prop at a time to its captive audience. First, a flotilla of nattering seagulls. Next, a rowboat at its mooring. Farther out, two lobster boats heading toward the sea. Finally, the vast pine forests of Westside Oyster Bay. Snapping the lid of his water bottle, Dan splashed some over his springy curls before sucking it dry. Suddenly, startled by a deafening clang, Dan whirled his head around to see a vagrant rummaging through the metal trash bins. Watching him, Dan's own fragility was abruptly laid bare – the summer spent wallowing in his own misery, overcome by feelings of worthlessness, his dignity lost in the bottom of a rum bottle. He watched in silence as the man fingered bits of trash from the bin, greedy seagulls landing at his feet. How had Dan escaped the fate of this unfortunate soul? Where and when is that point of no return, and how close had Dan come to that point? Did this man once have a home and family? Livelihood? What set him on this path of self-destruction? Addiction, betrayal, broken heart? Having unearthed not a morsel in the bin, the man gave it a powerful kick, cursed, and vanished. The gulls lurked for a moment longer, double-checked each and every napkin and wrapper the man had thrown to the ground, then squawking their grievances, lifted to the sky. Overcome with emotion, Dan walked home, shaken with thoughts of what might have been.

Back at the apartment, Dan was surprised and somewhat annoyed at the number of messages flashing. Mopping sweat from his forehead, he hit PLAY.

BEEP – "Hey, Tim here, property manager. Just checking up. Any problems with phone or internet, give a call. 822-3100."

BEEP – "Hey, Dan? Gem here. Is this still your number? I mean, are you still in town? Leevon and I are gonna brave the winter here when the campground closes after Labour Day. Renting one of the new Cranberry Motel apartments. 445-2101."

BEEP – "Hi, Dan. Desi MacLeod. Time for another chinwag? Give me a call. No rush."

BEEP – "I miss the seagulls, Danny." Dan's heart skipped a beat.

Karla misses the seagulls. That can mean only one thing… and she called me Danny.

Gaping at the phone, he began to pace. Circling it like a shark. Fists clenched. Resentment rising.

Yah? Well, guess what. I miss my son. Ever think of that? Ever think of that?

Glaring at the phone and wringing his hands, he continued

to circle.

She called me Danny.

A lump was forming in his throat as he dialed his in-laws. "Mildred? Is Karla there? I'm returning her call."

"Dan," she said softly. "She's gone to the dentist. She'll be a few hours. You doing okay, dear?"

"Come again? You've been blowing me off for over a month, so why the sudden interest in my well-being? Just tell her I called back."

Dan saved the other messages, and called Desiree.

***

The waitress at the Hava Java observed with interest as Desi and Dan awkwardly shook hands, chose a corner table and were seated. When their coffees were poured, Dan watched in horror as Desiree emptied four sugar packets into her mug.

"Any luck selling your house, Dan?"

"No lookers yet, but still early days. On a happier note, I just unpacked the last box in my new apartment, down there at the old Cranberry Bog Motel."

"Hey, I hear those apartments are quite nice."

"Very nice, spacious."

"I've got my parents' house on the market too, but like you, no serious lookers."

"So—"

"So—"

The conversation stumbled sideways.

"Sorry, you go first."

"No… you"

This has to be a first date thought the waitress, as she

approached the table with curiosity. "You two have enough creamers there?" she asked.

"We're fine," Desiree smiled.

"Yah, we're good, thanks," Dan agreed.

Desiree's thumb circled the rim of her coffee cup. "This is my Oyster Bay day. I spend Wednesdays out here trying to launch the new food bank on Bayshore Drive. My Port Sherman facility seems to run itself, I have great volunteers there. But here… well things were off to a great start, then everything went belly up. Doing my best to salvage what support I had, but it's a hell of a battle. I'm quite sure I know who's screwing me over."

Dan fidgeted uncomfortably in his seat, and Desiree picked up on his anxiety. "No, Dan! Sorry, I'm not trolling for volunteers," she laughed.

Dan's forehead relaxed. "That's good, because what I need is a paying job".

Desiree had been somewhat intrigued with this ruggedly handsome, apparently single, sincere and witty man who she had met under the most bizarre of circumstances. She could always read people well, but she couldn't quite place into context this new acquaintance of hers. Now a wall was coming down.

"Unemployed?"

"Ruined," he said.

"Wanna share? I'm a great listener. Big ears, small mouth, short memory."

Dan glanced around the cafe. People moved about noisily, clinking spoons and scraping chairs. The palms of his hands massaged his sculpted knees. He studied her face for a moment, and sucked in a slow breath.

"It all started one morning at church."

***

The waitress prowled about their table. The lunch crowd would soon be pushing through, and these two have been hogging a table since ten a.m. It was one heck of a discussion, whatever it was. Their voices rose in squawks and squeals and swooped down in whispers.

"I cannot believe this!" said Desiree. "The Friar has been royally jerking both of us around. For months! And I know without a doubt he's the cause of my food bank delays!" cried Desiree slumping back in her chair. "And he's killed any chance of you ever becoming a nurse, or ever working again in the hospital, in any capacity?" Twisting his napkin, Dan only nodded. Sensing that he had shared enough of his personal woes, Desiree changed the subject.

"So where were we… on the ashes story, last time we met?"

"Um… your dad finding his King Eider. The keel falling off in his workshop. Your mother's note for her friend. But I'm still waiting to hear how the ashes ended up inside the damned bird."

"Well, now, that's the fun part. You see, it appears the Reverend Terrence Fry, in all his holiness, removed Dad's remains from his marble urn moments before the funeral, pretended to bury them and then slipped the ashes to Mom in a cardboard box."

"When?"

"Right after the burial. Before we even left the cemetery."

Dan rumpled his brow. "And the ashes landed inside the decoy how?"

"My mom was no slouch in the workshop."

Dan took a moment to process the information. "Un-bloody-believable," he said. "Let me get this straight. The Friar buried an empty urn in front of everyone?"

"Uh-huh."

Dan's thoughts ran wild. The Friar had been the cause of everything – the suicide of Lucy Halliburton, Dan's dismissal from the hospital, Archie's ashes and the unsettling events at the house, the departure of Karla and Matthew. He steepled his fingers and focused on the wall behind Desiree's head.

Should I tell her about Archie's presence around the house, his reflection in the window that night? The mysterious grey dust always scattered around the hearth where the decoy sat? Should I tell her about all that?

The waitress drifted silently toward their table. "Anything else, folks?"

"No," said Desiree impatiently. She too was deep in thought and bursting at the seams.

Should I tell him what else I know about the Friar? No, it's not my place... but Alan could. Yes, he'd have to hear it straight from Alan. He's on duty until one. We still have time to catch him.

The waitress stood by as Desi stood up and punched her fists into her cardigan. "Be sure to check out that article in *Christ Chronicles*. It's on the church website. No wonder my project's gone tits up. I'll never get this food bank off the ground."

At the cash register, Desiree said, "I'll take what's left of the morning muffins, please."

The cashier gave a blank stare. "All of them?"

"Please," said Desiree.

"You're hungry?" asked Dan.

"No, but others are," she replied.

Dan held open the plate glass door. "So, Dan," she said as she ducked under his arm, "we should write a book about the

Friar and all his dastardly deeds."

"Ashes, Ashes, All Fall Down?" Dan's blue eyes danced. The puzzled waitress watched as the pair of them, laughing hysterically, stepped out into the sunlight.

"Dan, which way are you walking? I'm heading down Bayshore Drive to dust my empty food shelves for the hundredth time. Come with me. There's someone I'd like you to meet."

"Promise you won't recruit me."

"You're safe. C'mon."

Alan's biceps strained under the sleeves of his denim shirt, as he sat picking through a mountain of paperwork – a sifting of silver through his hair the only indication of his age. His eyes remained fixed on his work as Dan and Desi stepped in from the sidewalk.

"Any sign of the operating permit yet, Al?" Desi asked.

Alan's lips parted in response, but he stopped short when he saw Dan.

"It's okay. This is my friend, Dan Duggan. I've been bending his ear all morning about our start-up delays. The permit?"

Alan sighed. "I've been tormenting the pants off them at Town Planning, but they keep giving me the brush-off. They say it has to go before the Regulations Committee. Again!"

"Where are we on the wheelchair ramp?"

"Now, it's two inches too close to the sidewalk."

"And the fire exit?"

"Doesn't meet fire code now. Too far from the fire hydrant."

"Health inspector?"

"On three weeks holiday."

"See?" Desiree said to Dan. "One month ago, we were all set to go. Now all this nonsense."

"Oh," said Alan, "and next week's door-to-door food drive

is cancelled, and I just found out FreshMart removed all their drop-off bins."

"It certainly looks like you've been shoveling shit against the tide, doesn't it?" said Dan.

"Sure does," said Desiree. "Say, Alan? Suppose you could tell Dan what you told me? You know, that business about the Friar?"

"Oh, that guy," he sighed. "Well, like I told you, Desi, the investigation is closed, no charges were laid, and I'm retired from the police force, so I guess there's no harm in me discussing it. I just wouldn't want it... you know, broadcast or spread around."

Dan attempted to appear only half-interested, but curiosity sparked in his eyes. "Landed himself in hot water, did he?" he asked.

"It was a few years back. A group of church people filed a police report. The Friar had accused each one of them of stealing stuff from the church. These people were like, you know, the janitor, the caretaker, a couple ladies on the guild... the ladies who polish the brass and silver. Anyway, according to their report, whenever something went missing from the church, he would accuse one of them, so they started following him home and, sure enough, he was hauling the goods into his basement apartment."

"So, that's proof, right? Proof enough that it was him swiping the stuff?"

"Well... not really. No video or photographs were ever taken, so it was their word against his. But we questioned his landlord and, sure enough, he backed up the police report. He confirmed the apartment was packed to the ceiling with crates of sacramental wine, and semi-precious metals, like brass communion chalices, crosses, even a few silver offering plates."

"Offering plates!"

"Yup, and we didn't need a search warrant. The Friar was more than happy to consent to the search. The place was a bloody mess. He was one of those hoarder types, you know. And he stood there all pompous and arrogant, claiming he bought everything at various flea markets over the years, online sales, even received them as gifts. It was a real piss off. We just couldn't nail him. And he had one heck of a church treasurer, I can tell you that. She could spin a story, that one."

Desiree was about to interject, but decided this was not the time to inform Alan and Dan that her mother, Alice MacLeod, was that loyal church treasurer, who so eloquently spun those tales.

Alan inhaled deeply. "Anyway, it was the box of gold and silver pieces that really clinched it for us."

"Pieces? What do you mean pieces? Like coins? Jewellery?"

"No, more like residue, all melted, if you know what I mean… all tossed together with twisted bits of what looked like dental appliances."

Dan shot Desi a questioning look.

"He's talking about gold and silver tooth fillings, Dan," she said, "from cremated human remains."

Dan's eyes grew wide. "That's grave robbing."

"Oh, at its finest," replied Alan, "and we couldn't get him on a damned thing."

CHAPTER 34

"Aunt Annie!" Desiree squealed. "You look so much like Mom!" At the baggage carousel, Desiree tried her best not to gawk at her mother's ghost.

Annie fussed and fiddled with her purse and carry-on bag. "Well, honey, we are identical twins, after all... or WERE, I should say," she added quickly. "You look simply marvellous, my dear. I detect a hint of Archie in you, but you can't take blame for that. Ha! ha!" Annie gave her niece a tight squeeze. "Oh my, but it must have been hard, dear, losing your mom so soon after your dad."

"It was, Annie. It was tough. But now I'm looking forward to some one-on-one quality time with my favorite aunt."

Annie shot Desiree a quizzical look. "Last time I checked, I was your only aunt."

With a pout, Desiree replied "Small family, aren't we?"

"Indeed we are, my dear, and shrinking by the moment... oh, here they come." Annie's two oversized suitcases emblazoned with travel stickers came whisking around the corner on the belt. In one swift movement, Desiree grabbed them and heaved the bulging bags onto the luggage cart. "Let's get you home," she said.

***

With all the grace of a twenty-ton steamroller, Annie settled into

Desiree's spartan apartment in downtown Port Sherman. "You live in Boston. Not Mongolia. Why are we such strangers?" asked Desiree.

"Terrible, isn't it? And the sad thing is, we can't get those years back, so let's make the most of this visit. Any more of that wine?"

"My dear lady, there's enough wine in that cupboard to drown a sailor."

"Excellent. Now where were we... oh yes, the high school prom, ha! ha!" she cackled. "Oh, your poor mother's dress!" The rim of Annie's wineglass was greasy with lipstick, and her travel-weary eyes ringed in mascara when she finally hiccupped her way to bed.

Desiree was exhausted and wondered if she could keep up with the old dame for another four weeks. "G'night Annie," she said softly through the guestroom door, but all she heard was the rumble of a locomotive racing through the room.

***

By week's end, Annie had scoured and shopped every crevice in downtown Port Sherman. After one such exhausting shopping adventure, she entered the foyer of Desiree's condo building with her visitor's key, hobbled to the elevator on her high-heeled Saint Laurents, dropped her bags and hit the UP arrow for the fifth floor. Moments later, from inside the apartment, Desiree heard her aunt puffing along the corridor and when she finally tripped through the door, Desiree called out to her. "I'm home, Annie! Don't want to startle you!"

"Oh!" she huffed. "You home?" Her words came in breathless spurts. "Why aren't you... out dating some...

handsome young man on this… gorgeous Saturday afternoon?"

Desiree sat with a bandaged ankle resting on the loveseat, and a bag of frozen broccoli held to her eye. "Funny you should ask, Annie! Does 'hit by a forklift' answer your question?" Annie's faced dropped when she entered the room.

"Whatever happened?" she croaked. "Forklift! Where? In the warehouse? Oh, my goodness, dear. Look at your eye!"

"I'm fine, really. Just a sprained ankle and a few cuts and scrapes. No broken bones on X-ray. My foot got trapped and twisted under one of the forks and I was knocked sideways. Luckily, it's my left foot, so I can still drive the car."

"But, Desiree! Why were you working on a Saturday?"

"Ten pallets of potatoes were coming in, and I had to open the cargo bay. The forklift operator was newly licensed and, let's just say, a bit eager."

"Here. Let's get you into bed."

"No, Annie, seriously. I'm fine. Look, I gotta prepare a speech for tonight's fundraiser."

"You can't speak on that ankle! It looks like a-a… a cooked ham!"

"Annie. It's the Shriners. Big event. I'm going. Now, can you order us a pizza and keep down the chatter?" Annie, somewhat offended, whisked through to the kitchen and plucked the Pizza Palace two-for-one coupon from beneath its magnet on the refrigerator. "Would the delivery of a 20-inch Veggie Delight make too much noise for you, princess?"

Ignoring the sarcasm, Desiree popped an Ibuprofen, and began brainstorming her speech from her favorite perch five storeys up from Granton Lane. An additional $175 per month would have afforded her a bird's eye view of the showy entrances of the trendy pubs and restaurants on Empire Street, but Desiree was far happier watching over the one-way thoroughfare that snaked its way through the jumble of rear delivery doors that supplied the restaurant kitchens. Granton Lane and its clanking dumpsters crawled with activity day and night.

It's too bad you never got it, Dad. Seven years of study and what does your daughter do? She hands out free food. Free groceries for bums. Never mind all that touchy-feely business of social inequality, child malnutrition, education disparity. They're all just freeloading immigrants and drugged-up teenagers. Yes, Dad. Non-humans crawling through dumpsters for an untouched dinner roll, a half tub of coleslaw.

"So, you've got your Sociology degree now and your Masters in Public... what's it called?" Archie had asked at her graduation lunch.

"Health," Dad said. "Masters in Public Health."

"Yah yah. But what's the career plan?"

"Humanitarian work."

"No, silly girl! I mean, what will you do for a living?"

"Humanitarian work that pays."

"Somewhat of the classic oxymoron," he said. "You should have taken science like me."

Hmmm. Now that's not a bad theme, actually. Not bad at all.

Now, with creative juices flowing, Desiree began jotting down her speaker notes. *Putting a Stop to Hunger – No Science Required.*

***

The following day, Annie prepared her signature Sunday dinner and, as she cleared away the dishes, Desiree dropped onto her sofa with her laptop. "That was delicious Annie, thank you!" she hollered to the kitchen. "Chicken Kiev. Wow. Way better than the Shriner's spread last night!"

Annie stepped into the living room and gingerly perched herself on the arm of a chair. After an agonizing silence, she dropped it like a lit match. "She never told you, did she?"

Desiree lifted her face from the screen. "Hmm?"

"Your mom, she never told you. About the half-brother."

"Whose half-brother?"

"Yours."

Desiree eyeballed the near empty wineglass clutched in Annie's arthritic fingers. "How many of those have you had?"

"It's not the wine talking, dear."

Desiree's eyes dropped back to the screen. "Well, it's insanity talking, then."

Annie's wine glass listed dangerously toward the floor. "She always meant to tell you, but she died so suddenly, and—"

"All righty then, Annie, let's hear it!" Desiree snatched her glasses from her nose, and slammed down the laptop lid. "And hold nothing back! You've lifted the rock. Crawl on out."

Annie cleared her voice and began. "He was born two years before you and put up for adoption. Your mother had a little, ah, indiscretion. Actually, she called it a moment of sheer and utter madness. A young theology student… a transient. He had a troubled childhood. Your mom took him under her wing."

Desiree frowned and shook her head. "Two years before me? Do the math, Annie. That's impossible. She was already married to Dad."

"Desi, this isn't easy for me. Do you want to know or not?"

"Well, jeez!" Desiree laughed. "We're kinda at that point-of-no-return, don't you think?"

"Your father was away a lot. Out there on that godforsaken sandbank, what's it called?"

"Baggs Island."

"Yah, that place. She would've never married a meteorologist if she'd known the nature of the beast." Annie emptied her glass with a slurp. "Anyway. It was while your father was out there beachcombing and playing with weather balloons, and God knows what else, that the child was conceived."

"Can we skip that part? The dirty deed part? I get it, okay? I get it."

"Alright. When your father came home, he never suspected a thing. But your mother was beginning to show."

"Nope! Bad dream. Someone stick me with a needle."

"Abortions were frowned upon in those days and not easily arranged, so she was in quite a predicament. Desiree dear, you would NOT believe how close she came to telling your father." Desiree sat rigidly on the sofa, fingers picking at the upholstery, eyes burning holes in the floor. "But guess what!" Annie continued. "By the grace of God, Hurricane Beulah took out all your father's transmitters, and he had to skedaddle back out there. This time for three whole months! So, your mother decided to continue with the pregnancy. She spent her third trimester with me in Boston. The baby was born at Mass General... you all right, dear? Wait, I'll get you some water."

Desiree watched in stunned disbelief as her aunt breezed through to the kitchen as though the world hadn't just, moments ago, shuddered on its axis.

"So, where has this mystical half-brother been all my life?"

"Boston, with his adoptive parents. Until they both drowned. Very tragic. On his fifteenth birthday. He was passed around child protective services for a while, then ran off. Wandered his way up here to Nova Scotia with nothing but a dog, a wrinkled photograph, and all his adoption records, bearing your mother's name, of course. He wasn't the brightest candle on the cake, but he knew how to navigate the system."

"Well, how do you know so much about him? Hell. You don't know that much about ME!"

"Oh, for Heaven's sake, Desiree. He came knocking on her door, okay? Shocked the bejesus out of her. Told her the whole tragic story of his parents. She phoned me in Boston, in a total panic – asked if I'd ever heard of the double drowning in Boston Harbour. I had actually recalled something years before, but of course, had no idea who the people were. I contacted the Boston Globe. They sent me a copy of the article. I brought it for you. It's in my suitcase."

"Pardon me, Annie, for taking a few moments to process this... this TV documentary."

"Anyway, the boy wasn't expecting to find his father here too, but he did. Yep, he sure did, poor kid," Annie said shaking her head. "Anyway, Desiree, your half-brother's name is Willy, and he lives somewhere in Oyster Bay."

Desiree's face softened. "Annie. Please. My brother lives an hour's drive away? You can't be serious."

"I'm afraid I am, honey."

"Does he know about me?"

"Oh yes, indeed he does! But your mom always kept you two apart. Mind you, his volunteering at HungerStop had her a bit on edge, but he promised to keep quiet. He and your mother lived in close proximity for the past two years."

"Unbelievable. Mom knew this guy was working alongside me? I want to strangle her, except she's dead already. Did Dad ever find out about all this?"

"Never."

"Did Sully know?"

"No one knew."

Desiree rose from the sofa, and limped her way about the room, hand held protectively to her black eye, fuming, twisting and twirling clumps of hair. "Where can I find him?"

"Last I heard from your mother, he was in a trailer somewhere in Westside Oyster Bay." Annie made a casual sweep of her hand. "Somewhere... I don't know, somewhere up the road from her church."

"Way-way-WAIT!!" Desiree raised the palm of her hand to Annie's face, her heart tightening in her chest. "The trailer... the burned-out trailer." Desiree moved to the window, forcing panic down her throat. With her back still turned to Annie, she said, "I already know this guy, Willy. Now, who's the father?" said Desiree.

"As I said, dear, he was a foreign theology student when he came to your mother's church, many moons ago. He had childhood issues. Your mother was a listening ear and a shoulder to cry on. He was one of those... what are they called... a travelling deacon, or some such thing."

Outside the window, a gathering of grey clouds moved reluctantly through the polluted skies of downtown Port Sherman. "Sweet of you to drop this bomb on me now," she said sourly.

"Desiree, I'm doing my best. This wasn't my job to tell you. This was well and truly dumped on me. Is there any more of that wine?" she asked, twisting her head to the kitchen.

"No. No more wine. Who's the father?"

Annie's empty glass landed with a clink on the table. "He moved back here to work nine years ago. I thought your mother's anxiety would go through the roof. Try to imagine it, Desiree. Secretly giving birth in another country, years later the biological father drops back in town, then the kid comes a-knocking! Your mother had no choice but to tell the father. He was none too pleased at the news, I can tell you that, and plays no part in Willy's life. None. Zero. Zilch."

"For the last time, Annie."

Her aunt remained silent for a moment. Desiree turned her bruised and swollen eye to face her, and watched in horror as the words dripped like battery acid from Annie's ruby lips. "That dreadful Terry Fry," she said.

***

At the BuyGones junk shop, old Gert waited patiently as Willy splashed fresh water into her chewed plastic bowl. She turned her clouded eyes to the sound of the approaching vehicle. Desiree's head bobbed and weaved as she navigated the potholed parking lot. Willy stood fixed in his spot, his nicotine-stained fingers fidgeting with the water jug.

Maybe she's still looking for that... thing... whatever it was.

He lifted his battered ball cap, smoothed his mop of sandy hair and twisted it back on. The old retriever slobbered water over the verandah boards as Desiree's two crutches exited the driver's door. Willy watched in puzzled silence as she propped each one in an armpit, propelled herself across the rough terrain, and stopped at the verandah stairs.

"I never knew," she said.

CHAPTER 35

"Where are we doing this?" Annie asked.

"I have the perfect place in mind," replied Desiree, gazing deeply into her cell phone.

"What are you looking at?"

"The driving directions."

"Will we have to walk any distance? Because I would need to change my shoes."

"Shush, Annie, let me read."

"What's the forecast? Will I need a jacket?"

"Annie, please. Just a second."

"Can I carry the bag?"

"YES! You can carry the bag! Okay, here it is. 'Bistro LeCoq'. Beautifully restored French Manor and Bistro, specializing in traditional Provencal cuisine. Open Daily eleven a.m. to nine p.m. You ready? Let's go," said Desiree, "and yah, grab a jacket and lose the heels."

Desiree plucked her sunglasses from the overhead compartment, and she and Aunt Annie rolled out onto the highway heading inland to higher and drier ground. She recalled a phone conversation with her mother.

"*You must see the place, Desi. It's lovely. So authentic and —*"

"Keep it short, Mom."

"*I know, dear. You're busy. But the menu... oh, and the grounds are beautiful. Will you come with me sometime? Your* father's not too keen on the place. We ordered the Soup du Jour and it was a lovely tomato bisque, but served with a baguette and goat cheese and, well, you know, your father would rather lick an ashtray than eat anything goat."

"Oh, the poor guy. I suppose that ruined his day, did it? He can be such a sookie, Mom. I'll take you there someday, okay? But right now, I gotta go."

"It was built in eighteen-something. A stone manor, so quaint, with a clay-tile roof, wrought-iron grates in the windows, wooden shutters. The lady who runs it, her great-grandfather came over from France and built it. He grew up in Provence, I think... anyway, they also grow grapes for a nearby winery. You know the winery with the French name in the valley... I forget now, but you know that nice local wine. What's it called?"

"Darned if I know."

"And such a beautiful view of the lake from the dining room... and the sheep! Did I mention the sheep? Magical."

Now with overwhelming feelings of guilt and regret, Desiree reached over and tenderly touched the burgundy velvet bag in Annie's clutches. The simple wooden sign on the roadside read: *BISTRO LECOQ, Next Left*. A newly-graveled driveway wound its way through a stand of white birch and the graceful grounds stretched out on either side. Gardens of plush, purple lavender released their fragrance under the morning sun. The French tricolor flapped a friendly greeting atop the flagpole and the sun-bleached stone house sat quietly on a small rise of land. Desiree pulled into the parking lot and turned to face Annie in the passenger seat. "You ready, Champ? Let's do this." She turned off the ignition, pocketed the keys, slid from the driver's seat and walked around to the passenger side to help Annie. "Here, pass me the bag," she said.

"But you said I could carry it."

"You can! Just pass it to me while I take your hand." After much fuss and fuming, Annie was eventually tugged from the car, landing on two feet in the gravel.

Desiree looked in horror at her feet. "What the HELL are those!"

"What do they look like? Slippers."

"Why didn't you wear walking shoes?"

"Ladies from Boston don't own such hideous footwear. Now let's go. I'm fine." Arm in arm, they made their way to the dining room doors. Through the windows, Desiree watched two young employees flip white linen tablecloths up and over the tables as she and Annie waited by the entrance. A bespectacled lady appeared at the door.

"Very sorry," she said glancing at her watch. "Our dining room doesn't open for another hour."

"We've just come to take a look around if you don't mind," said Annie.

The lady peeled off her apron. "I'm afraid I can't let you in until eleven."

"Oh, that's fine. We won't be coming in for lunch. My mother told me all about this place before she died. She loved it here," said Desiree. "The menu, of course! But especially the property and its history." Desiree's eyes scanned the landscape. "It's so lovely here," she gushed. "My mother was also quite taken with the sheep. May we take a walk across the fields?"

"Yes, yes of course. You'll find a lane leading to a bench overlooking the lake. You won't be bothered by our sheep farmer. He's at auction today, but yes, please, go. Enjoy your walk." After a momentary frown and grimace at Annie's fluffy pink feet, the woman closed the door. Desiree and Annie followed the crumbling stone wall along the pebble lane. Touching the smoothness of each stone and the cool fuzziness of the moss beneath her fingers, Desiree picked her way downhill – Annie stumbling and pressing the velvet bag to her chest.

"Why couldn't we just bury your mother in the cemetery?" Annie panted. "There's mud here. And sheep shit."

Desiree stopped and leaned against the clammy stone wall. "Well, here's the thing," she said, "Dad's not in the cemetery, is he? Mom made sure of that. And, according to her infamous note, she wasn't thrilled about being planted in the cold ground either, so why put her there? I found the receipts, okay? All of them. Receipts for the double burial plot, receipts for the funeral, receipts for the marble urn, receipts for the bogus burial. Nope. No more dealings with the Friar, the church, or the cemetery. Dad's brass plaque is still on the phoney grave, I've added Mom's name to it, and it's staying there. No way he's gonna resell that double plot, and no way he's gonna dig up that very expensive and, may I add, very empty, marble urn. I'll visit the cemetery with flowers and wreaths and plastic butterflies, and whatever good daughters do. Now c'mon, keep walking, slow poke."

Annie grumbled and griped all the way to the wooden bench but, as the two sat down on the bench, a hush fell upon them. The beguiling scene, just as Alice had described, settled around them like a soft blanket. Like images in Bible stories and nursery rhymes, flocks of sheep dotted the landscape, quietly grazing on the gentle hillsides overlooking a sparkling lake.

"Oh, Mom," Desiree sighed. "Magical, indeed." She sat for a few moments, then looked back to the Bistro. The breeze gently rustled the flag in the direction of the lake. With glistening eyes, Desiree took the velvet bag from her aunt, loosened the pull string, lifted it into the air and held it upside down. Alice's billowy remains, caught in a gentle updraft, drifted silently over the pasture, over the backs of the soft and woolly creatures, across the water and into the dazzling light.

***

It had been somewhat of a silent drive home, but once the two women were settled back within the arms of urban comfort, clothes were changed, lunch was prepared, and conversation picked up as though it had never dropped.

"Can I keep the bag?" Annie asked, peeling a cucumber.

Desiree slid a cutting board in her direction. "Of course, Annie. I can't think of a better keepsake for you to take home, nor can I think of anyone I'd rather have with me today. I couldn't have done it without you." She pulled the block of cheese from the refrigerator. "I see you found some clean slippers. The muddy ones are going straight in the trash, you know."

"Fine with me," Annie shrugged. "Less to lug home."

Desiree let out a sigh. "I'm so gonna miss you. Hey, can you make that Chicken Kiev again?"

"Today?"

"Tomorrow. We're having company." Annie pushed the cucumber into the salad bowl.

"The handsome fella who had the decoy?"

Desiree straightened the placemats. "No, silly! WILLY!"

CHAPTER 36

Unbeknownst to Annie, Desiree had, just days before, breezed into the BuyGones store and informed her half-brother he was coming to supper. "This is not an invitation. It's an order," she laughed. "I'll come pick you up.".

Willy furrowed his brow. "Nah, I don't think so, thanks. Because, what about Gert?"

"Bring her! It's a pet-friendly building."

Willy rubbed his forearm. "Ah no. I don't really go anywhere no more."

"Willy. We're siblings. It's weird, I know, but you've known longer than I've known, right? So, you've had time to get used to it. Your biological aunt is in town, but she's leaving in a couple weeks. Our mother's twin sister. You'll love her. She's doing all the cooking, so we won't have to lift a finger. Please come." Gert's tailed thumped in agreement.

"What time?"

"How about three-thirty?"

Reluctantly, Willy replied, "We'll be ready."

***

Having survived her first-ever elevator ride, a skittish Gert was the first through the apartment door. Willy followed struggling with the leash, and in the rear was Desiree, grinning ear to ear. Annie wiped her hands on her apron and extended a hand. "You must be Willy," she said.

"Pleased... pleased to meet you," he said. Willy robotically reached to his head to remove the ballcap he'd abandoned while waiting for Desi. The circular depression in his thick hair, however, provided clear evidence of its being.

"And this must be Bert!" Annie crowed.

"Gert," said Willy. He snapped off the leash. The exhausted dog landed in a heap on the floor. "Stay now, girl," he said. Looking to Annie, he added, "She won't be no bother." Standing awkwardly clutching two cans of dog food, Willy moved aside as Desi navigated around both him and the dog.

"Here we are!" she said triumphantly. "We made it! This place smells heavenly, Annie!" Once all the shoes were kicked off, jackets were shed, and a water bowl was filled for Gert, Willy wandered to the living room window.

"You're up pretty high here. I can see the smoke stacks at the refinery."

"Yep. It's a much nicer view on a clear day though. You can see straight out the harbor."

"Is that HungerStop way over there? The green roof?"

"The Distribution Centre? Yes. A ten-minute bike ride from here."

"Willy!" hollered Annie from the kitchen. "What's your poison? Can I get you a beer?"

"Um... no, thank you, Annie."

"A soda?" she shouted.

Willy turned a puzzled face to the voice. "Soda?"

"Yah," she said, yanking open the refrigerator door. "Coke, Sprite or flat ginger ale?"

"Coke, please." Turning to Desiree, he whispered, "Is she American? People up here call it pop."

"Indeed, she is, Willy. Bostonian, like yourself."

Willy shot a bewildered look into the kitchen. "Huh? All them years I lived in Boston, and I had an aunt there?"

Annie stripped off her apron and stepped into the living room. Placing a can of Coke in Willy's hand, she said "The rice will be another thirty minutes. Let's all sit. Time for a talk."

Willy handed the can back to Annie. "Maybe I'll take that beer, if you don't mind."

To Desiree's relief, Annie spoke gently in relaying to Willy the details of his beginnings – hitherto shrouded in secrecy. Willy sat in polite silence, picking strips of label from his bottle of Keith's. "But why did my mother move way up here, after having me way down there?"

"Well, that's the part you didn't know, Willy," Annie said. "This was her home. She lived here in Nova Scotia all her life. We were both born here, but I left in my twenties."

Willy took a minute to let that sink in. "Did you know me down there?"

"Of course not, dear. I attended your birth, then you were legally adopted into a loving family. I could have no contact." The kitchen timer marked the perfect place to pause the conversation.

***

Table etiquette aside, supper went without a hitch. Gert devoured two cans of dog food from a plastic container, spilled water over the floor, and managed to remain on all fours for an entire twenty minutes before collapsing again on the mat beside the door.

"So, where were we?" asked Desiree as she eased herself onto the sofa with her coffee.

"Willy's birth and adoption," said Annie, "and I think we've covered it. Now, can we talk about that 'Desiree' tattoo?"

"Oh, this?" Willy rubbed his arm. "Well see, I met this guy on the street who was learnin' to be a tattoo artist. He needed people to practice on, so I thought why not. First, I asked for a GERT tattoo but he wanted to practice more letters. He said don't ya have a girlfriend or sister with a longer name? I said yah but I can't spell it, so I called your mother... our mother."

Desiree beamed with delight. "Yup! I remember seeing it at the distribution centre. You were off-loading pallets with your sleeves rolled up. Stopped me dead in my tracks. That's such a great story, Willy!" She reached across and touched her brother's knee. "Any others you'd like to share with us? Or questions you'd like to ask?"

Willy scratched his head and leaned forward, elbows on his knees. Fixing his gaze to the opposite wall, he began, "Well... I mean..." Annie and Desiree waited patiently, giving Willy all the time he needed to gather his thoughts. Rubbing his chin, he began again. "Like... I... um..." Silence lay like an itchy blanket over the room. Finally, from around the corner, old Gert let one rip, breaking the silence with what began as a high-pitch squeak, building in volume as it blew through her bowels, groaning to a deafening blast. "BreeeaaAAARRPP!" Willy's eyebrows shot to the ceiling. A crooked grin spread across his face – his pink gums gleamed in the candlelight. "GOOD ONE, GERTIE!" he howled, slapping his knees. "Ha! Ha! You should hear her after a corn dog!" And it seemed somehow, at that moment – at the fart of a dog – that barriers were broken, walls came down, the playing field was leveled. The same blood coursed through the veins of this hapless trio whether they were acutely aware of it or not.

"My cheeks are sore from laughing!" cried Desiree.

Willy gave his sister a shove. "Ha! Not as sore as Gert's, I bet!"

"Where's that leash? said Annie. "Me and Bertie Boy are going for a walk. Blow the stink off us. You two kids get to know one another."

Desiree followed her aunt from the room. "Should I show him the Boston Globe clipping?" she whispered.

"Oh dear, yes. He should be encouraged to talk about his parents. It's the elephant in the room now, isn't it? See if he'll open up."

Willy appeared in the doorway. "Open up about what?"

"Oh…" Desiree flushed. "Your parents. About what happened all those years ago."

Willy froze. "We should be gittin' home now," he said. "Thank you kindly for the chicken kee… the chicken supper." Gert struggled to her feet beside the door.

"Please stay," said Desiree. "We have a news clipping here. About the accident. I'd like to know about your parents, Willy. I feel attached to them in some way." Annie snapped the leash on Gert's collar and, despite some initial confusion, the dog offered no resistance. Out the door they went. Desiree scraped two kitchen chairs from beneath the table. "If this is too painful, Willy, it's okay. We can just leave it. Never speak of it again."

Willy slumped into a chair. "What does it say?"

Desiree reached for the clipping from atop the refrigerator and slid her glasses from her head. "Two Bodies Recovered from Boston Harbour after Family Fishing Accident."

Willy propped his elbows on the kitchen table and dropped his forehead into the palms of his hands. "Read me the rest."

"You sure?"

"Keep readin'."

"Divers recovered the bodies of a man and woman, both in their fifties, who drowned in a bizarre incident involving the hazardous stowage of rope on a government wharf. The couple leave behind a fifteen-year-old son who was also at the scene. Massachusetts State Police have launched an investigation to determine the cause of the tragedy. No charges have yet been laid."

"Let me see it," said Willy.

Desiree slid the clipping across the table, as shock and sadness gripped his face. "That's MY picture," he said. "That's mine. They used my picture."

Desiree smoothed a finger across the three grinning faces in the black-and-white photo. "You all look so happy. When was this taken?"

"Right before it happened. Right there on the wharf." With stubby fingers, Willy pawed the clipping from the table and shook his head. "It just ain't right. That's mine."

"Who shot the photo, Willy?"

"Jemila. She took it on mom's camera."

"Who's Jemila?"

"The black lady. She sent me the picture when I was in foster care. She wrote me for a few years, but then she musta died."

"Did Jemila have a last name?"

"No. I mean, yah. But I couldn't read it. It was long. Went right across the envelope."

"Okay. Ready for a nightcap?"

Willy squinted at the clipping and blinked away tears. "Sure. Whatever a nightcap is." By the time Annie and Gert came bursting through the door, Desiree and Willy had made inroads, but barely scratched the surface of his childhood. Desiree had learned something of his beloved parents, their inspiring work ethic, their modest, fun-loving existence, and their hopes and dreams for their son.

***

After driving Willy home, Desiree returned after midnight to find her aunt waiting up for her. "Fair to say the evening went well," Annie said.

"Yah. I think so," she replied, tossing her car keys on the counter. "We had a good gab on the way home. He told me about the day he met his sperm donor. Did Mom ever tell you about taking Willy to meet him?"

"No. She didn't. Put the kettle on."

"Let me get into my jammies," Desiree said. Annie pulled the fleece throw across her knees and was beginning to doze off when Desiree returned with two mugs of tea.

"Okay," sighed Desiree. "So. Why Mom chose such a crappy day to do this, I'll never know, but anyway, she and Willy knocked on the church vestry door one day in the pouring rain. They knew the Friar was inside because his vehicle was there. Willy said he didn't want to meet him but Mom insisted. When the Friar heard the knock, he parted the drapes and then swished them shut, like angrily, Willy said. Mom knocked again but Willy wanted to leave. All of a sudden, the door swung open, and the jerk just stood there, glaring at Mom. Didn't even glance in Willy's direction."

"What an ass," said Annie.

"Yah, Willy said the rain was pouring off the brim of his ballcap, and Mom couldn't keep her hood up it was blowing that hard. Finally, the Friar says 'I told you never to bring him here.' Mom said 'Can we please just step inside? He came all this way.

All the way from Boston'."

Annie sipped loudly on her tea. "Did he let them in?"

"Nope. Willy says the Friar still hadn't looked in his direction when he said to Mom, 'I don't owe that person anything. I didn't know he existed until last week. And now you expect me to do what? Get together for a picnic and throw the ball around? Teach him to change a tire?' "

"Hah! Like he could change a tire."

"I know, right? Or throw a ball! Anyway, Willy started backing away from the door, but the Friar stepped outside, grabbed Willy's cap and literally tore it off his head."

"What the...?"

"I know. Poor Willy just stood there dumbfounded, and so did Mom. Then he threw the cap in a puddle and said to Willy. 'I needed to see your face, just the once, you understand, numbskull?' Willy said 'Okay.' Then the bastard said 'And I don't want the misfortune of seeing it a second time!' and he slammed the door in their faces."

Deep in thought, Annie fingered the warm mug. "And all those years in Boston, I thought I was the high-wheeling twin. Alice saw way more action up here in these godforsaken woods."

CHAPTER 37

Dan spied the notice in the grocery store:

CHURCH OF THE HOLY TRINITY FUNDRAISER
Lobster Dinner and Silent Auction
Keynote Speaker: The Reverend Terrence Fry
Proceeds to Global Outreach Program
Dinner tickets $100
Silent Auction – Cash only
August 25, Parish Hall

"Global WHAT?" Dan said aloud.

The cashier swiped his card. "Outreach. Global Outreach. Supposed to be quite the event. I think the priest is going to Africa or some place." Dropping the groceries in a plastic bag, he added, "and I hear they're scoring some pretty amazing auction items."

Dan exited the automatic sliding doors like an angry wind. "Outreach, my arse" he muttered. "Likely story." Once home at his Cranberry Bog apartment, he poured himself a coffee, powered up his computer, brought up the church website and clicked the calendar. Sure enough. There it was. October 12: KENYA – Canadian Christian Ministries Conference. Dan swivelled his chair, picked up the phone and dialled Desi's number.

"Me?" she giggled. "Scarf down a hundred-dollar meal in aid of hungry children a world away? Don't think so, Dan. Bad optics. You going?"

Dan took a slurp of coffee. "Oh yah. That's one rodeo I won't miss."

A few moments later, Desiree phoned him back. "Dan, did you read this part? The CCM Conference is held at the luxury InterContinental Nairobi. The Friar won't be spooning up any bowls of porridge from that palace!"

"Not surprised," he scoffed.

"Listen, Dan, much as I don't wish to support this gig, I would love to buy tickets for my lobster-loving aunt and my half-brother. Maybe you could sit together?"

"Um, sure," he hesitated. "How will I know them?"

"Believe me, that won't be a problem. My brother will be the toothless guy, and my aunt the tipsy one with the ruby lipstick and Bostonian accent. I'll drop them off and pick them up. Let's just say, they'll liven up the place. Trust me on this."

"I'll find them," he said.

Deciding to undertake a bit of detective work, Dan hit the Registration tab on the CCMC website, but was unable to log in without a registration number. He dialled the toll-free number and asked for inquiries. Overjoyed to hear a friendly, unrecorded voice, he quickly grabbed a pen.

"Good afternoon, Canadian Christian Ministries. How may I help you?"

"Hello Ma'am," he stammered. "Very sorry to bother you. Reverend Terrence Fry speaking. I have a real predicament, I'm afraid."

"How may I help, Reverend Fry?"

"You see, today my laptop was stolen, and I've lost access to all my registration information, my entire itinerary, my sessions, my talks… I do apologize for the bother."

"Let me check the database. Terrence with a double R?"

Dan's tummy took a leap. This was way too easy. "Yes, double R."

"… and it's F.R.Y.?"

"That's correct." Nothing short of giddy now.

"Middle name, please?"

"Aw, shit," he mouthed to the ceiling.

"Hello?"

"N-no middle name."

"It's not James?"

"Oh, sorry. James, yes. There was a crackle on the line."

"One moment, please." Dan's teeth tore off a jagged strip of the thumbnail.

"Your registration number is CCMC223009."

"Thank you so much, Miss…?"

"I'm Gail Botha," she replied. "All my contact info is on the website under the Registration tab. Happy to help. I do hope your laptop is returned, Reverend Fry."

"Well, today has certainly restored my faith in miracles. Thank you again!" he cried.

***

Dan arrived early to browse the auction tables and was astounded at the generosity of the local sponsors. Gift packages valued in excess of $500 – weekend getaways, car rentals, season theatre tickets, yacht club memberships lined up along the first table .

The second table groaned under the weight of framed oil paintings, clay pottery, stone sculptures and wood carvings. Lesser items in the price range of fifty to hundred dollars included whale watching adventures, golf lessons, spa treatments, and restaurant vouchers.

The model schooner nearly dropped from Dan's fingers as the Friar approached. "Dan... Duggan, isn't it? Haven't seen you at church for a while. How wonderful to see you. My back is in fine repair, by the way! Angels, they are in the pain clinic, Angels!" He threw his arms to the Heavens. "How can I ever thank you?" he beamed.

"Oh, don't worry, Reverend, I'll think of something. You can count on it," Dan replied. The Friar lingered at Dan's side for a moment before gravitating away, somewhat rattled.

Dan had no problem identifying the man in the tuxedo standing near the bar, gumming down jumbo shrimp handfuls at a time. The sleeves of his threadbare jacket barely reached around his elbows, while the shirt cuffs were so long, they grazed his beefy knuckles. His pants, two inches too short, failed to hide his grey woollen work socks, and it wasn't until he wiped his mouth in two swipes – first with one wrist, then the other – that Dan beheld the pair of mismatched cufflinks that completed the outfit. "You must be Willy," Dan smiled warmly and extended his hand.

"Yup, that's me. You Dan?"

"Yes, a friend of Desiree's. Great to meet you, man. She didn't mention her brother would be so debonair," Dan smiled.

"Oh, the tux? Yup, got the whole thing at Frenchy's. Twenty bucks!" he beamed.

"And I'm Annie!" boomed an abrasive voice from behind. "There's a good table right up front there! Grab me a white wine. I'll hold the table!" Annie held three places at the circular dining table, as a cluster of well-mannered guests arranged themselves in the remaining seven chairs. Once all were seated, the customary nods and hasty introductions one would expect at such an event were offered around the table.

When the first course of cream of asparagus soup was placed in front of Willy, he tipped the bowl to his lips before the other table guests were served. Annie noisily cleared her throat, gestured for him to wait, then placed the soup spoon in his hand. Willy tried gallantly to keep his paws under the table while the lobster was being served, but his broken fingernails tore off a claw before the platter touched the tablecloth. His dinner companions grimaced politely at every guttural sound, elbows knocking the water glasses, chin glistening with warm butter.

While dessert was being served, the Women's Auxiliary collected the wads of cash and bidding forms from the auction tables, then headed to a corner where they huddled studiously with their cash box and calculators.

Willy peered curiously at his crème brûlée. "How come they burnt my pudding?" he asked, innocently searching the faces around the table for an honest explanation. Clumsily rising to his feet, he leaned in across the table, gaping into everyone's dessert dish. "They burnt them all!" he said. "And these dinner tickets weren't cheap!"

"Just sit down and eat it, Willy," said Annie. "And shush, they're making some announcements now." It was at that moment that Annie shuffled her chair around to face the podium, Dan noticed several guests staring at her, gesturing and confused, stricken at the sight of Alice's MacLeod's look-alike.

Reverend Fry tapped the microphone. "Ladies and Gentlemen," he began. A hush fell over the crowd. "The moment we've all been waiting for! Your generosity has ALMOST left me speechless!" he grinned. "Tonight, I am proud to say, we have raised – drum roll please – $18,454.23 for my new Global Outreach project!"

The crowd rose to its feet in uproarious applause. The Friar bowed and beamed, aglow in the glory, while two giggling children were trotted out struggling under the weight of a hefty jar of coins. Heaving the jar onto the podium, one child said, "For the children in Africa. From the Sunday school."

"We sold lemonade!" beamed the other, and there arose in the Parish Hall another deafening round of applause. Dan remained seated, eyes fixed on the Friar. Simmering. Unsmiling.

A white-haired gentleman at the next table raised his hand. "Reverend, my wife and I have recently visited Kenya, and we feel extremely honored this evening to support your mission. Can you tell us the villages you'll be visiting, and will tonight's proceeds go directly to the Feed the Children programs?"

"Ah," said the Friar as he slid on his spectacles and quickly leafed through his notes. "Let's see now... not quite sure of the village names... um, that might take a moment, and they're quite difficult to pronounce. Shall I get back to you on that? Oh, and the money will go... well not directly to, but ultimately yes, the food."

Another hand shot up. "Reverend, first may I say how much we – my entire family here at this table – admire your commitment to this missionary effort. We were wondering about the feeding stations. Are they held at orphanages, or schools, or are the local churches used for this purpose? Also, will you be billeted at the homes of the local pastors?"

Dan let out an audible snort.

"I do believe the feeding stations are, um... let me see now. In the schools." Nervously shuffling his papers, he muttered, "My itinerary has changed so many times."

The founder and CEO of Foxhill Golf and Country Club stood up at his table. "Reverend, my daughter here – stand up, honey – is studying the rising socio-economic crisis in Kenya and wishes to follow your travels as part of a school project. Will you have a travel blog? And will you journey out to the villages the morning after you arrive?"

Dan raised a finger in the air. "Reverend? May I help? The wine and cheese reception is your first obligation. On the Friday evening in the foyer of your hotel, the Five-Star Intercontinental Nairobi."

The Friar shot an annoyed look in Dan's direction. "Oh yes, thank you." He cleared his throat and continued. "Then Opening Remarks the following morning... let me see now." He fumbled furiously through his notes. "My apologies... one moment."

A heavy silence hung over the Parish Hall as Reverend Fry tugged nervously at his cleric collar. Another question from the crowd broke the silence. "Reverend, perhaps when you locate your itinerary, you can tell us if you'll be attending any conference workshops... on forming future collaborations and partnerships... especially in the area of building self-sufficiency in Kenyan communities, digging water wells, increasing agricultural productivity, education, nutrition...?"

Dan stood up. "Um, Reverend? I can answer that. You did not register for any workshops. The morning after you arrive, Saturday... um, yes, Saturday. That's your helicopter tour to Tanzania to view Mount Kilimanjaro. Dinner, dinner, let's see... Ah! Six p.m. at the Tanzanian Wildlife Sanctuary."

A murmur fell over the crowd. The Friar stared at his papers, unable to articulate a single word.

"Then, on Sunday," said Dan, holding a finger in the air, "You will board your air-conditioned van for your safari. Sunset dinner that evening is at the Grand Safari Park and Casino. Long excursion day. Wear layers of clothing, it says here." Dan's words rang out like gunshots across the parish hall.

The Friar stood red-faced, trying to regain composure, and said quietly, "Yes, then Monday is my half-day of meetings. I'll meet Bishop Mwangi and he will be giving a talk on, um…"

"Oh, here it is, Reverend." Dan waved a sheet of paper. "Your one mandatory excursion. Tuesday, you visit the village of Wycarbunga. Population 320, fifteen miles west of Nairobi. Photo opportunities are as follows."

The Friar tried to interrupt but, like a driving rain, Dan continued. "$20 will buy you an 8 x 10 color photo of yourself surrounded by the village children. $50 gets you a video of yourself spooning porridge into their hungry mouths, and $100 will get you the photo, the video, and a framed certificate inscribed: Reverend Terrence Fry, CCMC Missionary of God. This doesn't leave you much time to board your flight home, Reverend." Like a news anchor, Dan straightened and tapped his papers on the table, clasped his hands and smiled.

Visibly humiliated, the Friar's eyes darted momentarily, first to the crowd, then to Dan's table, and he spotted Annie. The room began to spin as he steadied himself at the podium. The crowd followed his gaze. "I… ah… eh-hem," he coughed. Scoffing down a glass of Cabernet, Alice's twin glanced about the hall, oblivious to the stares, a high-heeled shoe dangling from her big toe.

The Friar forged ahead. "Are there any more questions?" he asked meekly. Peering over his glasses, he scanned the room. A palpable tension hung in the air as the crowd followed his gaze to Dan's table once again. The Reverend clutched frantically at the podium with both hands, the blood vessels in his neck about to burst. For there sat Willy, the scourge of his existence, feasting under the same roof, his dessert spoon tink-tink-tinking at the bottom of his dessert dish, deafening the Friar to all other sounds.

The Reverend wobbled. The crowd gasped. The town councilor stumbled from his table and hurried to the podium. "Bugger off, and let go of me!" the Friar hissed. Then, supported at the elbow, he recovered from his second shock of the evening.

"Must be the heat," grinned the councilor. "Yes, he's all right now, yes, just the heat," he assured the crowd.

The Friar's voice was weak. "If there are no more questions, I'll leave you to your desserts and coffee. I wish to thank everyone for—" the Friar stopped mid-sentence as his turbulent evening came to a grinding halt. Like party balloons slowly losing air and drifting aimlessly across the floor, guests gravitated to the coat rack, lugging their purchases, rattling car keys, making small talk, "must get home, the babysitter, the early morning, the fog, the dog." Members of the planning committee lingered briefly for their moment of acknowledgement with the Friar, but he was too distracted, craning his neck to ensure Alice's disturbing look-alike and his vagrant son had exited the building. Then, rushing the few remaining guests through the door with a "Good night, wonderful to see you this evening, thank you for your support," he tried to slither away. His grey suit was now rumpled and stained with perspiration, and he spotted the one remaining guest. The Reverend crooned across the empty hall. "Waiting for a drive home, Dan?"

"Waiting to walk you back to your office with that heavy cash box," Dan replied.

"Oh, no need! I'm quite capable!" he sang gaily.

"I insist," said Dan. "Let's go."

The Friar fumbled with his coat and keys, and when the door slammed behind them, they crossed the parking lot in stony silence to the church. As they stepped into the Friar's office, Dan recalled in blazing colour his last visit. "What, no filthy mug of cold tea?" he quipped. He dragged a chair to the desk. The Friar's mouth was a grim line as he eased himself into his armchair.

"What in bloody hell do you want?" he asked.

"Justice. Shall I explain?"

"Oh, spare me the good Samaritan act, Duggan. It's been a long night."

"I'll get straight to the point. You do realize I caused the postponement of a very sick patient in order to fast track your appointment at the pain clinic."

"My, but that's a rather healthy dose of self-importance you have there, office boy."

Dan pulled Lucy Halliburton's tattered obituary from the pocket of his sport jacket. "This is the lady," he said, sliding the paper across the desk.

The Friar scanned a few lines, and dramatically pressed a pulpy hand to his heart. "Oh, dear me," he mocked. "She died. How unspeakably sad. Now, is there a Part Two to this gripping story?"

"Thirty-three years old. Lived in a trailer home outside Port Sherman. Had a husband and two little boys. Couldn't endure her pain another day. She took her own life."

"While I do enjoy a good drama, this one lacks a certain, shall we say… point." The Friar smirked. "Are you so daft as to think I'm to blame?"

"Nope. I'm responsible." Dan folded the obituary and slipped it back in his pocket. "Oh, and thanks to the outright lie you fed Doc Durling when you showed up at clinic, the case was brought before the Disciplinary Committee, and I am now forever blacklisted with the university, the hospital, the nursing school. Shall I go on?"

"Please do. Watching a grown man cry can be ever so entertaining." The Friar leaned forward across the desk and clasped his hands together. "No? Not going to cry? Pity. Your wretched wife cries for me every Wednesday."

Dan struggled to remain calm. "Give me tonight's proceeds," he said quietly, "in the form of a cheque made payable to Hunger Stop."

The Friar's upper lip twitched as the smirk drained from his face. "In your wildest dreams, you bloody moron. Rub two brain cells together. Who the hell do you think you're dealing with here?"

Dan very slowly and deliberately slid across the desk the photograph he'd secretly taken at the casino poker table. "Oh, I know exactly who I'm dealing with here, but does the diocese?" The Friar gaped at the photo, turned a pulsating shade of crimson, and rubbed furiously at the back of his neck.

"Who the hell shot this?" he demanded. "What I do in my personal time is my damned business! You can't blackmail me with that! The diocese!" he snarled, veins bulging under the starched collar. "They'd never fall for a stunt like this!" Dan smiled at the Friar's spittle gathering at the corners of his mouth.

"Okay," Dan shrugged, "if the Diocese is so impartial to your activities, they probably won't give a hoot about that other business either…"

"What other business?"

"Archie MacLeod's ashes." The Friar's face then drained of all expression – his respirations loud and laboured. Dan continued. "Interfering with human remains is an indictable offence, Reverend. Following his death, Archie MacLeod's remains were the property of the executor – in this case Desiree MacLeod – not Alice, his widow."

The Friar shot up from his chair and shoved his face into Dan's. "That was a personal and private arrangement between me and Alice MacLeod. PRIVATE!" Wheezing and heaving, he slammed his fist on the table. Sour breath hung in the air. Dan remained silent. The Friar held his ground, defiantly staring him down, beads of sweat glistening on his upper lip.

Dan smiled. "Maximum penalty of $2,500, that is, according to Section 12, Subsection 1 of the Provincial Legislation Pertaining to Storage and Disposal of Cremated Remains and—"

"Don't you DARE lecture me, you jackass." Like a caged animal, he paced circles around the office, scheming an impossible escape. "How am I to explain the loss of over eighteen thousand dollars in funds?" he croaked.

"Yah, I hear ya. Where's an epiphany when you need one, eh?" Dan said, then added cheerily, "But hey, the funds won't be lost! They'll be… redirected!"

"In case you missed the point tonight," he choked, "I have a CCM Conference to attend in Africa!"

"NO REVEREND!" Dan sprung to his feet. "You have an all-expenses-paid VACATION to attend in Africa!" he shouted.

The Friar's underarms were saturated as he lumbered to the door. In the adjoining room, what sounded like the heavy door of a metal safe clanked shut. His lower lip trembled as he puffed his way back to his desk and flung himself into his leather armchair. The silver serpent curled tightly to the topaz gemstone as the Friar's fingers gripped the pen. Huffing, he angrily scratched out the cheque in the amount of $18,454.23, payable to Hunger Stop. "You'll live to regret—"

"Just sign the fucking thing," said Dan, "oh, and about that heavy jar of coins…"

"Don't push your luck, asshole," he hissed. Rising from his chair, the Friar slammed the cheque into Dan's chest. "Now listen to me, you wanker," he snarled. "If I ever see your face again, I'll have you run out of Oyster Bay like a scalded cat."

CHAPTER 38

Desiree tapped lightly on Annie's bedroom door before entering. Crossing the floor to the window, she swished open the drapes. "What a lovely day for flying!" she cried.

Annie groaned and shielded her eyes to the rising sun burning its way across her bed. "And here I was hoping it was the Jehovah's," she rasped.

"Up and at it, my dear. Airport at nine."

"Is that bacon I smell?"

"Yup!" Desiree threw Annie's robe over the bedpost. "Chop chop."

Annie rolled to her side and grunted to a sitting position. Her two swollen feet dangled childlike over the bedside. "Must you sound so eager to bulldoze me out of here?" she asked.

Desiree sat down beside her aunt and squeezed her tightly around the shoulders. "Annie, I will miss you like a severed arm. I cannot bear to see you go. I'm just trying to keep things light, you know?"

"I know, dearie," Annie yawned and patted her on the knee. "Me too. Now get that bacon on the plate with two over easies, and scoot out of my way. Don't you know I have a plane to catch at nine?"

After breakfast, the women returned to the guest bedroom. Desiree frowned at the two oversized suitcases sitting in a state of emergency on the bed. "We can't possibly zipper those," she said.

"You sit on them," shrugged Annie. "I'll zip."

"No! You need to repack," she said impatiently. "And what's this envelope? Is this going in your purse or what?" Desiree glanced around the room for Annie's prized Louis Vuitton.

"Oh that. Just a gift card I bought at the silent auction last weekend. It's for you."

An apologetic smile spread across her face. "Aw, Auntie. You shouldn't have." Desiree slid the card from its envelope. *Dinner for Two. Bistro LeCoq. Join us in our lakeside dining room for an evening of authentic French cuisine and fine wines, followed by dessert and liqueurs in a nineteenth-century French parlour.*

"Wow!" Wide-eyed with delight, Desiree gathered Annie in her arms. "This is so wonderful, so thoughtful, so… so… Oh my God, I'm gonna cry."

Annie wriggled from her grasp and sniffed. "Enough of that now. Let's get this show on the road." And with that, they re-folded, re-rolled, and re-stuffed each and every item in Annie's bags until the lids, stretched to bursting, were painstakingly zippered down. At the airport, Desiree said, "Thanks again for the splendid gift card. I think I'll take Willy as my guest."

"I thought you might. Just don't order the crème brûlée, dear. Now where's my passport… oh and do you have my e-ticket? Oh. Here it is. Yes." She pivoted her bags around to the check-in desk. "Now dear, how are you going to spend the rest of this sunny Sunday?"

"I think I'll take a jaunt over Westside to weed mom's perennial gardens. They're a mess."

"Whew," said Annie. "What a perfect day for me to skip town!" They laughed, hugged one last time, and Desiree watched her crazy aunt check her bags and disappear through security.

***

An unfurnished house is difficult to sell. The realtor's words were now ringing true, but Desiree was in no rush to sell her childhood home. The notion of hiring a gardener had, however, crossed her mind once or twice. Desiree squeezed into her rubber boots, grabbed the spade and trowel from her mother's greenhouse, and tackled the tangle of weeds strangling the delphiniums. Next door, the parking lot of the Church of the Holy Trinity was entirely deserted. She peered at her watch.

That's odd. Almost eleven o'clock. Time for family service. Where are all the minivans and scrubbed-up kids?

The irony, she thought. Hadn't she once told her mom the Friar had the soul of an empty parking lot? She plunged her spade deep into the soil, stood back and listened intently for the familiar clang of the church bells, but the only sound coming from the belfry was the cry of hungry crows.

Well, well. Nothing short of an earthquake would cause the Friar to cancel a service. I wonder what's up.

The hours passed quickly, and it was late in the afternoon when Desiree shook off her muddy work gloves and boots. Now, fully convinced she hadn't inherited one ounce of her mother's love of the soil, Desiree headed back to her Port Sherman apartment. But first, a quick nip into Westside Pharmacy.

Desiree slid a box of "Nightshade" hair colour along the counter to the cashier.

"Will that be all?" asked the girl.

Desiree stood transfixed at the checkout, staring at the newsstand. She read the headline twice. An image, once lost in her memory, now reappearing. The day of her mother's memorial. Out behind the parish hall. A dented roasting pan on the ground. A yellow liquid.

"Ma'am? Will that be all?"

"Hmm? Oh, and this," she replied, snatching the issue of the Bay Bulletin from the stand. When Desiree reached her vehicle, she flattened the newspaper across the engine bonnet, slapping down the pages in the breeze. It took a moment for the headline to sink in.

Anglican priest convicted in antifreeze poisonings of three Westside dogs. Sentenced to two years in prison.

CHAPTER 39

Sitting in the new flat, Dan waited nervously for Karla and Matthew to arrive. He checked the plastic wrap on the sandwiches in the refrigerator and turned off the burner under the pot of soup. Every shelf and cupboard was fully stocked with their favorite food and drink. The dozen boxes of Kraft Dinner would surely put a smile on Matt's face. He waited outside on the asphalt parking lot, which was to be torn up in a week's time to be replaced by sod and shrubbery. He prayed the noise of the heavy equipment wouldn't be too annoying for Karla. He walked out to the curb and watched for her car. He wondered if Matthew realized that Leevon was staying the winter – right here at the Cranberry Bog apartments. Bonus!

Dan and Karla's phone conversation, though somewhat transactional, had been warm and affectionate, with regret and apology on both sides, each pledging a commitment to start over, for the sake of their marriage, for the sake of their son. To take things slowly, to rebuild in a spirit of sobriety and honesty. To nest, once again, together in Oyster Bay. Having served the time penalty for job termination, Dan's unemployment insurance benefits had now begun, and the first payment was used for rental deposit.

Here they are!

Giddy with excitement, Dan smoothed his T-shirt in two quick swipes. The compact Honda hatchback pulled into the lot and Dan realized his heart was racing. Matthew climbed from the passenger seat and without closing the door, flung himself into his father's arms.

"Dad! I missed ya. I missed ya like crazy!"

"Me too, son," he said huskily. "I've missed you too."

Matthew hurdled through the apartment door. Karla fussed with her purse, keys, sunglasses, phone, and finally emerged from the car. Dan waited to assess her face. It was unreadable. She looked wonderful – her hair short and shiny, bouncing about her shoulders. His heart melted. "Karla, honey," he said. She walked toward him and wrapped her arms around his middle – the air between them alive again.

"If you'll have me, I'm ready to try this again," she whispered against his chest, and her words fell like a soft blanket at the bottom of his heart.

"Will I have you?" he murmured. "I'll never let you out of my sight." Together they stepped inside onto the lush carpet.

Matthew was already spread-eagled on his double bed. "Awesome, dude! This place is the bomb! Is this my room?" Springing to his feet, he slid the mirrored closet door and hollered, "YUP! That's all my stuff in there! Right on, Dad! And my own TV!" he yelped. Matthew leaped back onto the bed and started jumping up and down. "Is there Wi-Fi?"

"Of course, there's Wi-Fi." His father smiled.

"Yo! My own desk! Mom, go get all my game gear in the car!"

His eye scanned every electrical socket. The bedside tables. The dresser. The bookcase. "Hey, Dad! Where's my goldfish?"

"Goldfish Heaven. Nice place. Google it."

Karla's eyes traced every inch of every wall of every room. Fingering baseboards in search of dust, flipping mattresses in search of bedbugs.

"Karla, my dear. It's not a motel any more."

"I know, but those bugs can live in the walls for a year without a single blood meal. I saw it on the Discovery Channel." She ran her fingers along the bookcase. "My Harlies," she said quietly. She opened the oven door. "Good size, I guess." She poked around in the bathroom. "Bit small, but okay, I guess."

Dan stood, hands clasped in front of him, rocking heel to toe, as if awaiting an inspection sticker. Matthew was obviously overjoyed with the new digs, but Karla... well, she was hard to read. Dan watched intently. There appeared to be a slight tease of a smile on her face, but a disturbing and unmistakable pinch between her eyebrows. Karla raked her fingers through her stylish new bob, leaned back against the kitchen counter and crossed her arms.

Uh-oh.

"It's okay, I guess," she said, "but where will we put the crib?"

TWO YEARS LATER

CHAPTER 40

"DIRTY WIDOWS" it read. Willy leaned on his broom on the sidewalk, frowning at the juvenile scrawl across the grimy plate glass window. He shot a glance up and down Bayshore Drive before spotting them across the street, smirking in the shadows of their ballcaps. "Hey!" he hollered. "Who done this?" Snickering, the boys ran off, as Willy wiped the window with his shirt sleeve. Stepping backwards into the street, he looked up. Morning was always the best time of day to admire the sign, just as the sun peeked over the neighbouring rooftops. "GOODWILLY'S KITCHEN" was celebrating its one-year anniversary. "I don't want no fuss," he had said to Desiree. "Just a cake. One of those big flat ones."

Willy had thrown his heart and soul into the soup kitchen. Situated next door to 'The Red Maple', Oyster Bay's new HungerStop food bank, he was able to keep in close touch with his sister on a daily basis. Together they had forged ahead, despite the naysayers, despite the red tape and due process. The situation was ideal, for whenever Willy was in quick need of a tin of kidney beans or a bag of noodles, he needed only to nip next door. Willy was gifted with his sister's work ethic – his modest income and enormous self-pride the only reward after a long, exhaustive day in the kitchen.

Willy missed some aspects of his former self, as he would never quite get accustomed to having dentures in his head, nor having to brush them, nor keep tabs on a pair of eyeglasses. Now, his slick new haircut meant no one would recognize him any more and he didn't necessarily see that as a good thing.

"Ahh, what a handsome devil," Desiree had said as the barber swept piles of sandy straw from the floor.

"But I don't look like me any more," Willy grumbled.

"Of course, you do, bro! You've just been renovated. Like on those TV home shows where they spruce up the windows and doors, install new roofing shingles... you know, while leaving the home's delightful character intact."

Smiling brightly, the barber walked Willy to the cash register. "That'll be $12.50," he said.

Willy ran his fingers through newly cropped hair. "Not a bad price, I guess," he said, "for a whole new roof."

***

Twenty minutes to opening time, and the windows were indeed dirty – filthy in fact. Desi had mentioned that just last week. Willy now regretted wiping off the graffiti. She would have delighted in the comical misspelling. Deciding to give the windows a quick sponge-down, he headed inside, clunked a metal pail in the sink and twisted the faucet. As the pail filled, he imagined his tiny mother washing eighteen windows, over all those years, in the spacious Westside bungalow he now called home. Groaning and perspiring, he carried the pail to the door, placed it on the sidewalk, then disappeared inside to fetch the step stool. "Damned kids," he grumbled when he heard the crash, but what lay before him when he returned to the sidewalk was not the work of mischievous children.

Willy fell to his knees. "You okay there, buddy?" he asked. The overturned pail rolled side to side, a river of soapy water spilled into the street, and an elderly man lay on his backside, propped on his elbows, on the ground.

"You try to kill all your customers?" the man barked, grunting and cursing himself to a standing position.

"Sorry. Just washing a few windows. Not open until nine."

"Try putting the opening time on your flyer," he muttered.

"Here, come inside," Willy said, helping him along. He led the injured man to a table. Shaken from the incident, Willy was never so happy to see his two energetic breakfast volunteers bursting through the screen door, all smiles as usual.

"When's the cake arriving, Will?" Matthew asked, donning his apron.

Leevon quickly flipped the OPEN sign and greeted the newcomer at the table. "Morning, Sir! How do you like your eggs? Boiled, fried, or smashed?" The surly man didn't bother to respond. "Okay, bacon and sausage ready in ten. You know the drill, right? Make your own toast, pour your own coffee, milk your own cow?" Unamused, the man shuffled to the coffee machine.

"Must be a drifter," Matthew whispered. "We don't know this guy, do we?"

As the regular breakfast crowd barged through the door, the ogre sliced into his sausage with the delicacy of a plastic surgeon. Willy glanced about the dining area. He hadn't seen anything vaguely resembling table manners for well over a year. The feeding frenzy was now underway – the rowdy, burping, jostling crowd – in stark contrast to the silent curmudgeon tediously sawing the crusts from his toast. His hands appeared to have never known a day's labour and Willy, in all his days, had never seen a bald head so wrinkled.

"Hey! You over dere," one of the regulars shouted. "You new

'round deez parts?"

"Drop dead," the man replied, eyes fixed on his plate.

"Hey, hey. Take it easy. Just bein' friendly!"

"You got a fish hook up yer arse, old man?" another chimed.

"Cod got yer tongue? Har Har!"

"Leave him alone, guys," Willy said. "He took a bad tumble outside this morning. You all right now, bud?"

The man wiped the sausage grease from his lips and raised his eyes to Willy's. "Go straight to hell, asshole," he snarled, and Willy felt a sudden chill run up his spine. Something brushed against the ridges of his memory – the oily eyes, the nippy show of teeth, like a testy dog you don't disturb while eating. Older now. Willy backed away cautiously as the man crossed the floor, spitting obscenities all the way to the door.

Later that afternoon, Willy scraped the remaining bits of icing from the cake platter. "I told Gem I didn't want no balloons, and no clown," he scowled. "But she came anyway, 'cuz nobody listens."

"Now, now, Willy," said Desiree. "The whole world knows Gem will find any excuse to hang out at Goodwilly's, am I right, Leevon?"

"Can't argue that!" he laughed.

A scarlet tinge rushed to Willy's cheeks and, in an effort to spare him further embarrassment, Matthew piped up, "Hey, Will! Who was that fella this morning? The guy with the attitude? Did you know him?"

"I didn't at first." Willy said. "But yah, I knew him all right, but he didn't recognize me."

"Well, who the heck is he?" asked Leevon.

"Not proud to say it, but he's my father."

***

Safely back in the muddled sanctity of his basement apartment, the Reverend stood horrified at his reflection as there'd been no full-length mirrors in prison. Gaunt and stooped. Ravaged. Body and soul. He hadn't anticipated that many dog lovers in the slammer. Nor had he anticipated the terror he'd felt earlier at the soup kitchen – his first foray into society. He balled his fists to quell the anger that constantly burned within.

His eyes roamed about the room. Everything had remained untouched over two years. A little dusty maybe. The bulging sack of unopened mail sat inside the door. He'd need to give the landlord a little something for that. Yes, a good chap was the landlord. And Sully, of course, for arranging the rent payments each month, although she hadn't bothered to visit the penitentiary in all that time. Stupid scarface.

Gingerly picking his way through his hoard – heaps of prayer books, collection envelopes, burial urns, piles of canned goods pilfered from food bins, UNICEF boxes bursting with pennies, Boy Scout collection tins, church bulletins, dirty clothing, litter and debris – he reached the tiny adjoining room. His holy place. His private shrine. He unhooked the red velvet rope at its entrance. The white satin altar cloth had yellowed along its edges, and the brass communion chalices were beginning to tarnish. Cobwebs sagged heavily between the candlesticks. On their wire coat hangers, his vestments hung from the hook on the wall. He flung a cape of musty satin about his shoulders. Heaving, he grasped a case of sacramental wine and dragged it across the floor toward him. He fingered for the corkscrew, still hiding in its place under the altar. Hopelessly out of practice, the Reverend cursed and struggled to dislodge the

corks, then filled the hefty silver flask to its brim with deep burgundy wine. Snatching the *Book of Common Prayer* from the altar, he fumbled with its bookmark and opened to the Holy Eucharist. His eyes flickered about the room.
You're home. You're safe.
He began his private sacrament. "*Almighty God. Unto whom all hearts are open, all desires known...*". His voice trailed off, as imaginary forms emerged from the shadows behind him – lurking, breathing over his shoulder, pressing their prison-clad bodies against his.
No one's here. Start over.
"*Almighty God, unto whom all hearts are open, all desires known, and from whom no secrets are hid—*".
A tremor began at the base of his spine, as sinister chuckles behind him rose to uproarious evil laughter. Terrified, the Friar shut the prayer book with a slam and, hugging the overflowing flask to his chest, fell to his knees, and surrendered to his demons.

***

The morning sun strained through the grubby basement apartment window. On the floor, the Reverend lay shuddering in a cold sweat, empty wine bottles lay askew, beside him the empty flask, its silver spout stained with the blood of Christ. In his chest, a powerful squeezing. In the distance, a siren wailing.

CHAPTER 41

On the bow of the boat, Karla elbowed her son. "Look, Matt. Look at your dad," she laughed. "He's like a guy in a beer commercial." Karla had been quietly observing her husband leaning back on the stern, elbows propped behind him on the aft rail, gazing skyward as the mainsail filled on a steady sou'wester. The 24-foot day-sailer had been purchased on Dan's fortieth birthday a few weeks earlier, and Karla was astounded at how skilled he had become since christening her. The *"Heart Song"* ploughed effortlessly through the sunlit swells of the bay, leaving a sudsy, green froth dancing in its wake.

Little Lucy Duggan sat securely in the circle of Matthew's arms. Her curly head sodden with sea spray, her chubby arms slick with sunscreen, and the lids of her pigeon-soft eyes beginning to droop.

"This thing's too small for her, Mom," Matt whined as he fiddled with a strap on her lifejacket.

"They're supposed to fit snugly," Karla laughed. "Stop fussing over your sister, pity's sake!"

Dan glanced at his watch and scanned the shoreline. "What say we head back, hey, guys?" he hollered up to the bow.

Matt nodded. "Yah, Lucy's getting tired."

Karla zipped the lid to the picnic cooler and gave Dan a salute. "Ready about, Captain."

"I knew you'd catch on to this, Matey," Dan laughed. "Tacking! Helms a lee!" Smoothly pushing the tiller away, he released the mainsail rope from its cleat. Matt and Lucy ducked their heads under the boom as the vessel came about.

"Again, Daddy, again!" Lucy cried. "Boom-Boom. Again!" The mainsail flapped noisily as Dan repositioned himself in the stern, braced his bare feet firmly against the gunwale, and leaned back tightly on the mainsail sheet. Like a finely-tuned instrument, *Heart Song*, on its new course, gracefully sped toward home on a close reach wind.

"Nice job, Dad," said Matthew. "Now hurry. Lucy's getting cold."

Karla rolled her eyes, and turned to Dan. "So, you all ready for tonight?" she asked.

"Yup… I guess. A bit nervous."

"You'll be a star," she said.

Matthew wrapped a towel around his baby sister and held her tight. "You gonna be a good girl tonight, Lucy Goosey?" Nodding, she snuggled into his warm chest for the smooth sail home.

CHAPTER 42

It was humid and sticky in the old auditorium of the Ocean Academy overlooking Town Centre, as the stackable chairs scraped the floor and people took to their seats. Halfway back in an aisle seat, Lucy was whipping up a second wind. "Where Daddeeee?" she wailed.

"Shh," whispered Matthew. "You'll see Daddy soon. Just wait." Karla stood in the shadows of the side aisle with her camera and telephoto lens. Matthew's grip encircled Lucy's tiny knees as she stood bouncing on his lap. "Make her sit," Karla mouthed.

"You need to be quiet while Daddy talks, okay?" Matthew always enjoyed the attention Lucy drew in a crowd, and he glanced around the auditorium for smiles and nods of approval. But tonight, everyone was focused on their programs, squirming in the heat with their phones and cameras.

On the stage, a double row of seats sat empty, and above them, a banner which read: *Congratulations EMTs and PARAMEDICS*. Lucy watched intently as the graduates took their seats onstage, followed by a group of instructors.

"Where Willy?" asked Lucy.

"He'll be here. Don't worry. Desi too. Just watch for them." Lucy hopped across to Karla's vacated seat. Kneeling backwards with eyes peeled to the auditorium doors, her razor-sharp baby teeth gnawed noisily at the wooden stackable chair. Matthew was overjoyed to see Willy and Desi wander in. Someone else could entertain the wiggle-worm for a while. Uncle Willy always managed to find a treat in one of his pockets, and Lucy soon settled on his lap with a packet of soda crackers.

The lights were dimmed as a hush fell over the crowd. Matthew thumbed through the pages of his program. The Opening Remarks were brief.

"…and it is my pleasure to now introduce tonight's Class Speaker, Mr. Dan Duggan. Come on out, Dan!"

To a round of applause, Dan crossed the stage in long strides and approached the podium. Karla's heart skipped a beat as he tapped the microphone. His rugged cheekbones touched by the day's sun paired handsomely with his dazzling blue eyes and gray linen sport jacket. She lifted her camera to her face and focused the lens.

"Good evening, Ladies and Gentlemen. For those of you who don't know me, I'm Poppy!"

A murmur of laughter drifted through the crowd.

"And that name has served me well over the past two years, as I suspect it's the reason I was chosen to speak at this evening's ceremony. I am truly humbled by the honour… and yes, I am old enough to have fathered most of my classmates.

First, I would like to thank our outstanding instructors, whose unwavering patience and skilful guidance has brought us here… to this momentous occasion. You have nurtured, encouraged, mentored, and counseled us through challenging times, stepping above and beyond the call at every turn. We are forever in your debt. I would also like to thank our Medical Director, Dr. William Russell, for his exceptional leadership. Finally, to our families and friends, we would not be here tonight without your undying love and support.

When I enrolled in this program, my life was in shambles. Today, I could not be a happier man, nor more fulfilled. Over the past two years, I have witnessed unspeakable joy, love, trauma, tragedy, braveness of heart and strength of spirit."

Dan paused for a moment, and looked to the faces of his fellow graduates. "I know I speak for us all when I say, Praise the Lord it's over!" Dan beamed. "We did it! With the help of one another, we made it! Our hearts and souls will forever be connected."

"You're making us cry, Poppy," chimed one of the graduates.

Dan cleared his throat. "But enough sentiment," he said. "I had an experience, just last week, that I would like to share with you – the experience that I feel marked the end of my training. The 911 call came in from a couple of teenaged girls, up to mischief on their way to school. They admitted to peeping through a basement apartment window and reported a man lying face down on the floor. They could not confirm he was breathing. Orlando and I were dispatched, and he was the driver, so you know how fast we got there, right?" Where did you train anyway, Orlando? Indianapolis? In the Ambulance 500?" Laughter erupted onstage as all eyes turned to the infamous instructor.

Dan continued. "We pulled up to the apartment door. I grabbed my drug bag, airway kit, threw the defibrillator onto the stretcher and ran. Law enforcement had already opened the door. I checked pulses, then rolled him over. A male in his early sixties, drifting in and out of consciousness. I checked the airway. Clear. Respirations shallow. Checked pupils, glucose, blood pressure; Orlando attached the EKG leads and as I was hooking up the monitor, the victim suddenly grabbed my sleeve, and for a split second our eyes locked in shock and disbelief."

Dan took a sip of water and looked to the crowd. "Ladies and gentlemen, that moment will remain imprinted on my memory for life. The victim and I were mortal enemies. Had been for many years and, for reasons I cannot explain, I was suddenly overwhelmed with desire to save his life. He was terrified. I was terrified. He went into V-fib, then cardiac arrest. I started chest compressions hard and fast. Orlando brought out the defibrillator paddles. We worked it for thirty minutes but, unfortunately, it was over.

We prepared the patient for transport, and I climbed in the back of the ambulance. It was sometime during that 150 kilometer-per-hour crazy ride on a bumpy road that it hit me hard – the simple truth. This man lying before me, who I had held responsible for all my trials and troubles, had not ruined me. He had simply diverted me – blown me off course – and although I was lost at sea for many dark months, I eventually adjusted my sails and discovered a new horizon. Where another life waited. An exciting life. This life. The paramedic life for which I was destined."

Dan lowered his gaze to the podium and shuffled his notes. "Tomorrow, we head out in separate directions, but we will always be a team, for no amount of geography can ever divide us. The same fire burns within us all." Dan looked to his classmates. "Yes, we will save lives. Yes, we will leave our mark on humanity, but most importantly, we will continue to strive for excellence. There are no second chances. Not for first responders. We need to get it right, the first time, every time." Dan loosened his tie, slipped his hands into his pockets, stepped out from behind the podium and addressed his fellow graduates.

"This calling of ours – this skill we now possess – is something we must never take for granted. Graduation is only a beginning. The real learning begins now. So, let's get out there. The world of emergency health awaits. Oh yes, and enjoy the remainder of the evening folks because this is the last night you'll ever be off duty!"

CHAPTER 43

"Stay in bed. The house is cold. Look at your story books."

"Is the oil truck coming, Daddy?"

"Just look at your books, okay? Or here... here's your LEGO." The man hastily dumped the plastic container across the boy's bed and lumbered out of the room.

Little Mikey Halliburton loved the oil truck. How he yearned to sit behind the steering wheel. Maybe the driver would let him again. Under the blankets, he listened intently for the comforting beep-beep-beep of the truck in reverse. His baby-blue eyes shifted to the window. Sometimes, when morning peeked through the curtains, he'd hear his mother's voice. Fading now from memory but he heard it, faintly still, and the sound of her shiny green jacket swishing when she walked. Mikey tried hard to remember both her smiles – the one she used when she waved to the mail lady, the laughing smile when her eyes would squint and her teeth would show; and the other one she used when her neck hurt, the sad one. Mikey waited for the oil truck until his empty tummy hurt, then crept out into the frigid gloom of the trailer home in search of his father. Unable to find him, he stepped outside. Hunkering down on the rickety verandah, his short rubber boots chafed his bare legs. His frayed pajama bottoms grazed the frosty step. He stared desolately across the littered yard, beneath the jacked-up truck, where grubby work boots gouged angrily in the mud.

"Hand me the big ratchet," his father growled from under the truck, as Mikey's older brother fumbled in the toolbox. Dad was always mad now.

A tattered, blue tarp tumbled and rolled aimlessly across the patchy lawn and hurled itself at the shed door. He remembered the day everyone came and whispered, and stared at the shed, carrying soup in big pots and rolls wrapped in tea towels. The shed where Mommy went that day. Before the square truck with the flashing light came. And ran over his bike.

Mikey's tiny buttocks were numb from cold when the car pulled into the rutted driveway. "Dad! The turkey man! The turkey man's here!" The boy's rubber boots thumped their way across the yard as Dan Duggan parked and reached into the backseat of his car for the hamper.

A muttered cuss word came from under the truck, and the work boots dug their way through the mud and gravel until the man wiggled his way out from underneath. Lying like a dead housefly on the ground, he grunted, "You again." He got to his feet and lit a cigarette. "Gotta say," he said, filling his lungs with smoke, "these boys of mine sure do look forward to you comin' each year." He looked at Dan quizzically. "Tell me again. How did we get on the list? And do you deliver to the whole neighbourhood?"

"Nope. This is my only delivery out to Port Sherman. Our foodbank serves mainly the Oyster Bay area."

"But why come way out here just for us?"

"What does it matter?" Dan smiled. "I like seeing the boys, and I'll keep coming as long as you'll let me. I've been through hard times myself. Sometimes a family just needs a break."

Mikey peered into the HungerStop Christmas hamper as his older brother leaned smiling against the truck.

"Are there candy canes?" Mikey squeaked.

"Yes," Dan smiled. "I made sure of that. Lots of candy canes."

"Chocolates?"

"Yep, and your favorite. Gingerbread cookies."

Dan poked around in the hamper. "Okay, so the turkey is a fresh one, so you'll probably need to freeze it. The vegetables are all grown in the Landsoe Valley. Cranberry sauce, the canned kind." Dan grinned and held up a cardboard package. "Stuffing is the Just-Add-Water type!" Mikey's eyes darted from hand to hamper. Dan continued to rummage. "Apples and oranges... let's see here... oh yes, the baked goods... all done by volunteers... oh, and don't tell anyone at HungerStop, but I tucked in a bottle of Christmas cheer for Dad."

The man spoke not a word but continued to suck noisily on his cigarette. A tired smile rumpled his face, as he watched his two boys drag the hamper to the house. "Take it inside, boys, and close the door behind ya," he shouted. Exhaling a cloud into the frosty air, he hacked and spit, and flicked his butt across the yard. "You got kids?" he asked.

"I do. A grown boy named Matthew, and a little girl – a chatterbox toddler named Lucy."

The man wiped his grimy hands down the front of his overalls and slapped his palm against Dan's. "I dunno how to thank you," he said, "but I can tell you this – it means a helluva lot. I just hope I can pay it forward some day, man."

Dan maintained his grip on the man's greasy paw. "I'm sure you will," he said with glistening eyes. Dan returned to his car, keyed the ignition, adjusted the rearview mirror, and shoved it into reverse. The man gestured for him to stop, and Dan rolled down his window.

"Yah?"

"Lucy was my wife's name," he said.

CHAPTER 44

From Bald Rock Point along the coast of northern Maine, Jacob, the lightkeeper, peered through his binoculars from his lofty perch in the lighthouse. On a clear day, Baggs Island, some twenty kilometers offshore, can be seen as a dark silhouette on the white horizon of the Atlantic. The overnight windstorm had heaped spidery piles of seaweed onto the pebbled beach below, and eight-year-old Meredith was combing through the rubble washed ashore.

"There she goes again," Jacob sighed as he placed his binoculars on the bench. "More wet shoes." He listened as she climbed the cast-iron spiral staircase to the watch room. Thunk. Thunk. Thunk. Jacob wondered what weird and wonderful treasures Meredith would spread across the bench this morning. Cold and shivering, she stumbled up onto the warm wooden floor.

"Look, Daddy. Look what I found," she panted. "How cool is this?"

Meredith passed him a duck hunting decoy, soggy with ocean water, worn clean of paint or other markings, smooth and cold to the touch. "Well, now, this here's a dandy!" Jacob said as he moved his gaze to the window. "Down there on the beach, was it?"

"Yes!" she replied. "It's heavy, huh?"

"Yep, it sure is. Probably full of sand. I've seen a few of these wash in over the years, but this one's quite well made. The keel's still in place. See?" Jacob ran his finger around the sturdy bead of glue. "Looks like someone's fixed it… reinforced it… with some glue and a couple of good screws," he said, puzzled.

"Can we keep it?" she asked.

Jacob looked fretfully at Meredith's collection of rocks, shells and starfish piled up on the window ledge. "Sure, we can," he said. "Now, is it a girl duck or a boy duck?"

"Mmm. I think it's a boy", she said, eyes aglow.

"Fine then. What say we sit him up here in the window? He can watch over Baggs Island. How's that?" he asked.

Meredith's tiny fingers were withered and white with cold as she reached up and stroked the decoy's head. "I'll visit you every day," she whispered.

***

Jacob's father had tended the light for thirty years and it was a foregone conclusion that Jacob would one day take over, that is, if the US Coast Guard was able to keep it in operation. Happily whistling about his chores, jotting notes in his logbook, Jacob faithfully observed the sea and sky, day and night. Sun flooded through the watch room, its rays bouncing in dazzling prisms off the massive lenses. The pleasing scent of sun-bleached timbers rose from the floor. Withered starfish and strands of seaweed shrivelled on the bench. As Jacob scanned the sea for signs of whale activity, a voice spoke up from somewhere along the window ledge.

"Hey, Jake, what's the marine forecast for today?"

Jolted from his reverie, Jacob dropped his binoculars and reached for the radio dials. No one on his frequency called him Jake. No one. Scanning back and forth through the channels and finding nothing but the usual radio noise, he quietly placed his coffee mug on the ledge and approached the staircase. "Is there someone down there?" he hollered.

"Just me. Over here."

Jacob turned his gaze to the voice – senses on high alert. His first thought was Meredith, the prankster that she is. But, of course, she was at school. His eyes darted along the window ledge. Could it be the conch shell from the Caribbean – they've been known to speak, or at least sigh like the ocean. He held the conch to his ear. The decoy sat baking in the sun. Jacob ran his fingers across its back. He picked up and turned over a few oyster shells and twisted hunks of driftwood, scanned the radio channels again and shrugged it off.

The job might be getting to me after all.

The following morning at sunrise, Jacob extinguished the light and climbed the spiral staircase to his watch room. It would be another hour before Meredith needed waking. He set the coffee on to brew before jotting the temperature, wind velocity and barometric pressure into his logbook. From which direction the voice came this time, Jacob could not determine.

"Must be magnificent out there on Baggs Island this morning. I used to work out there, you know."

Jacob dropped his pencil and jumped to his feet. Stalking the room, he yanked open the cabinet doors, dragged his desk away from the window, checked all connectors on the radio, but could find no explanation.

Gotta be a fisherman new to the area. A stranger to the airwaves. A real smart-ass.

Jacob returned to his house and his sleeping daughter, admittedly a bit rattled. First, he'd get Meredith up and off to school, then he'd ask around – see if there's someone new on the airwaves causing trouble.

***

My wood fibres are drying nicely on this sunny windowsill. I hear them crack and split from time to time. Aside from the noise of the foghorn, I reckon this is as good a resting place as any. I couldn't resist having a bit of fun with Jacob, but he's fine company and I won't bother him again. And that little Meredith. She's a doll, that one. Climbs all them stairs everyday and does her homework here on the bench. But she needs to work harder in science. She doesn't know her planets.

I didn't mean to upset that other family, the Duggans. I just had to get out of that house. That Karla woman cried the whole morning – the minute she found herself alone, she'd start. Bawling and blowing her nose, spreading out the blue baby clothes. Then she'd sit in her office and phone folks all afternoon, asking the same questions over and over. I think it was her job, but still. She asked more questions than my Alice ever did!

Now there was an old fool! My Alice. Did she really think a fella wouldn't notice the stretch marks? Or her sick and twisted relationship with the Friar? Did she think I didn't hear those whispered phone calls with whatcha-call-him? Her boy, the poor dimwit. Livin' like a hermit in that travel trailer, and her hauling plates of ham and potatoes up the road, and blueberry pies... for the church supper, she'd say. Likely story. I shouldn't have reported him, I know. He wouldn't have bothered them kids at the playground. But the fellas didn't rough him up too bad, and I made sure he wasn't home when I torched the place. And I don't feel bad.

I mean, folks do things – just look at Sully. My oh my, she got away with it again. First time she poisoned a mutt, she did it out back Mader's store. Then she snuffed three of them behind the *parish hall. Oh, she hated dogs, did Sully. But I can't say I blame her, with her face near chewed off as a kid. Oh, the shenanigans, but such is life, and here I am. Like I said, I don't feel bad. Crazy Alice never made me no blueberry pies.*

THE END